CAPTIVE

"Just because you're not in chains does not mean you are free..."

A Novel

Timothy Allen Smith

Published by

Twenty/20 Books

1108 Elmwood Avenue

Sharon Hill, Pennsylvania 19079

a division of

Twenty/20 Productions

Pasadena, CA.

Originally published by Twenty/20 Books in 2012

Printed in the United States of America.

This is a work of fiction. While, as in all fiction, the literary perceptions and insights are based on experience, all names, characters, places, and incidents are either products of the author's imagination or are used fictitiously. No reference to any real person is intended or should be inferred.

For:

Tai Juliette Wright-

(If there were only one thing I could wish for you, it would be for you to fearless in pursuit of your dreams)

Samantha Galltin-Wright-

(I honestly do not know what my life would be like without you)

Virginia Boyd-

(Everything I have ever done has been with you in mind)

CAPTIVE

Forward

To see men live...

One must first see men die.

To hear men laugh...

One must first hear men cry.

To feel true love...

One must first be stung by man's hate.

To accomplish anything even remotely worthwhile...

One must first aspire to achieve something great.

All men must Dream.

For, to man, to Dream is to be Alive...

When men don't Dream...

This is when men die.

-- Timothy Allen Smith

Prologue

For the life of him he couldn't understand why they played the music so loud. As long as they'd been coming here you'd think he'd have learned to deal with it, but it bothered him just as much today as the first time they set foot in the place. He complained about it constantly, to the point where even his friends were tired of hearing it. They begged him, on numerous occasions, to "let it go." or "get over it." He couldn't.

It wasn't like anyone was here to listen to the music. He'd asked the owner, the staff and even the DJ to turn down the volume, but they never did. Of course they would smile and assure him it would be taken care of right away, only nothing ever changed. He began to think they were doing it on purpose...and this made him hate them even more.

He smiled to himself at the thought. If they only knew how much he hated them and this disgusting place, but they didn't know. They couldn't know. Not yet anyway, that was the whole point.

"Yo Omer, you aint eatin?" his friend Xavier shouted over the music as he greedily tore into a plate of chicken wings.

"Nah, I'm good."

It wasn't that he wasn't hungry. There was just something about the whole strip club buffet thing that didn't work for him. Besides, he had other things on his mind tonight. Undeterred, Xavier stuffed his face "Man you better get in this. These wings is the truth!"

How anyone could even think of food in a place like this amazed him and, of all people, Xavier was the last person he would want to eat with, anywhere. The man actually seemed to enjoy speaking with food in his mouth. He wondered if his mother simply forgot to teach him any table manners or if he was just too damned stubborn to listen. Either way, watching him eat chicken in a room full of naked women was not something he was going to miss.

"Our package arrived this morning." he said calmly, the words stopping his friend mid chew. There was a long moment of silence between them before Xavier spoke.

"You sure?"

Omer reached into his shirt pocket, pulled out a small envelope and handed it over. As Xavier examined the contents, Omer had anticipated the confused look that came over his friends face.

"We do not get to pick the time or place."

Just then, their waitress arrived with their drinks. "You guys ok?" she asked as she placed two large glasses on the small table in front of them.

"Yeah we're good right now" Omer replied politely.

As she turned and walked away, Xavier picked up his glass and downed half of his draft beer in an instant. He put the glass down and went back to his plate of chicken wings.

"The others?" he mumbled through another mouth full of food.

"Their tickets arrived yesterday. We are all set."

After a moment, Omer stood up and began putting on his jacket.

"You leaving?"

"You should too. We have a big day tomorrow."

And with that, he made his way toward the door. Before he reached the exit, one of the dancers came up behind him and wrapped her arms around his waist.

"I know you not tryin to leave without giving me my love"

He paused for a moment and placed his hands on her forearms, gently massaging them back and forth. He leaned his head back into her and tried his best to melt into her arms, wanting to savor this moment for as long as he possibly could before speaking.

"I have to take off."

"You sure?" she said seductively. "It's dead in here tonight so I can give you some extra attention."

"I'm sorry baby. Got an early day tomorrow, but I'll check you out after work ok?"

"You promise?"

"I promise." he answered as he gave her a final hug and kiss on the cheek. When she left, he had to smile. The lie had rolled off his tongue so smoothly it surprised even him.

CHAPTER ONE

He chose a black Mercedes S550 sedan as his lead car. The ninety thousand dollar machine definitely seemed out of place when flanked by the much more modest vehicles carrying the rest of the funeral procession through the narrow streets of the city, but that was the point. He didn't see these people as his family and felt no need to blend in with them. He was only there to bury his mother and, once that was done, he planned on never seeing any of them again.

He couldn't have asked for better weather as he stood, head bowed, silently receiving the prayer of committal. The grass, still wet from yesterdays rain, had effectively turned his

Bruno Magli loafers into a pair of five hundred dollar Italian sponges and the sun, absent for most of his trip already, lay hidden beneath a massive bank of clouds forming directly overhead. The grey, ominous looking sky painted a perfect backdrop for the occasion, he thought. It was dreary. It was miserable. And, for Mark O'Connor, it matched his mood perfectly.

He closed his eyes and breathed deeply, allowing the unseasonably cool air to massage his lungs and take his mind away from the unpleasantness of the moment. His thoughts meandered back to a childhood of playing football with his friends not too far from where he was standing right now. He remembered being the smallest kid on his block and how much he hated being picked last whenever it came time to choose teams. Things were different now, he reminded himself. Now he was the one laughing last.

They'd walk home after those games, joking with each other about what kind of cars they would drive or what girls they would date when they were older. Looking back, it was comical how far his so-called friends had fallen short of those dreams. Dead end jobs and loveless marriages to frumpy, overweight women seemed to be the order of the day for the kids he grew up with, but not for Mark. For him, those dreams turned out to be much more than the whimsical musings of a pre-pubescent little boy. For him, they were prophetic...

"**My** god you look disgusting. Body dysmorphia my ass, Lisa Woodward you are FAT. And you are taking your fat ass to the gym TOMORROW."

It sounded good, in theory. The reality, she knew, would be a little different.

It wasn't that she had anything against physical activity. She actually enjoyed working out so working up a sweat was nothing new. What was new was her utter lack of motivation to do anything at all.

She didn't think it was depression as much as it was an honest reaction to what seemed like constant negativity bombarding her every sense. Barely a day went by anymore where the world wasn't introduced to yet another new catastrophe and you couldn't watch the news without getting the overwhelming impression that Armageddon, if not here already, was very near on the horizon.

So here she stood, a white, thirty-two year old middle school teacher from suburban Philadelphia, witness to the end of the world, and somehow she was supposed to find the motivation to lose that last five, ok maybe ten, pounds she needed to look like some twenty-something celebutard walking around on a beach in central America. Of course it didn't help that she would be walking said beach with mister ten percent body fat himself.

That thought elicited a slight smile. Leave it to her to fall for the only man in the school district with a waist size smaller than her own. She'd never been much into looks but there was no denying Walter, her boyfriend of over five years, was a beautiful man. A little more than six feet tall and a chiseled two hundred ten pounds, he looked like he stepped right off the page of a fitness magazine. He worked as a guidance counselor at her school and, in spite of his obvious physical gifts, what stood out most about him was his mind. She often referred to him as the smartest person she'd ever known and, what's more, he himself took infinitely more pride in his level of intelligence than in the impressive size of his biceps. For the first time in her life she was truly in love. As her eyes refocused on the image in the mirror, she felt her smile grow a little wider.

When the service was over, Mark instructed the driver to take he and his wife directly back to their hotel. He wanted nothing more than to get to their room, shut the blinds and sit blissfully in the dark waiting for this day to end. It had started to rain slightly and the rhythmic sound of the sedans twenty inch wheels spinning through wet asphalt had a soothing effect on him. He was completely lost in his own thoughts as their car wound past the auto mall and onto I95 going north, into the city. As they made their way toward downtown, he couldn't help but be disturbed at how out of place he felt. He had driven this route countless times and yet somehow he felt like a stranger in a foreign country. If it wasn't clear before, it was certainly clear now. His life, whatever it was when he lived here, was over. This would never again be his home and with his mother gone there was really only one piece of business left to handle before he could say goodbye to this place and move on with his life forever...that would have to wait until tomorrow.

CHAPTER TWO

The 1650 square foot presidential suite in the Loews Hotel, boasts two bathrooms, a formal dining room, and an amazing view of the Philadelphia skyline. The opulence, while admittedly over the top, had proven its worth many times over the years, especially when he felt the need to prove to someone how successful he had become. After all, few things sold success better than imported Egyptian linens.

Unfortunately, material success was the furthest thing from his mind at the moment. After staring at the ceiling for two hours, he'd finally given up on sleep and took refuge in a leather recliner by the window. He stared blankly out at the city, which seemed unusually busy for a Tuesday night, and began slowly recapping the days events. The funeral was only a few hours earlier and he was having trouble believing she was gone. There were so many things he would have said and done differently. So many things he would have liked to explain. Only now it was too late. This was a hard lesson but it was a lesson learned nonetheless. He put things off for too long because he always felt like he had plenty of time. He wasn't going to make that mistake again.

"You ok baby?"

He'd been so lost in thought he'd honestly forgotten Amber was in the room. But now, seeing her reflection in the window, he was instantly reminded how beautiful she was. A petite, natural red head with green eyes, perfect skin and an impeccable sense of style, she was the ideal arm candy for a young professional trying to portray a winning image; and if that's all she was, that would've been more than enough for him. But Amber was so much more than that.

"Mark?"

"Wha? Oh Yeah…I'm fine" he said, still staring out the window.

She looked over at the clock on the night stand and flopped back down onto their 300 thread count sheets. "Come back to bed…"

"Can't sleep"

"I know." she replied, propping herself up onto her elbows. "You were tossing and turning all night."

"Sorry about that…"

16

After a moment, she got out of bed and walked over to him. Knowing there was nothing she could say to make this day any easier, she at least wanted him to know he wasn't alone. She sat on his lap and began to gently caress the back of his head.

"Baby I know this is hard," she said, wiping fresh tears from the side of his face. "but your mother's in a better place now. You have to remember that."

Without replying, he laid his head onto her chest, closed his eyes and broke down in tears. Having never been the maternal type, she was surprised when she instinctively wrapped her arms around his shoulders and held him tightly. She knew not to waste time reassuring him. Now was not the time for that. Something inside told her she just needed to let him lean on her. This was all part of the process and, as much as it was killing her to see him in pain, she was relieved to see him opening up. Less than twelve hours earlier, the man had buried his mother and managed to hold it together throughout the entire process. Now it was his turn to be a mess and it was her job to be there for him. She sat on his lap, holding him until they both fell asleep.

He woke up to the sound of the shower running. Now alone in his chair, the first thing he noticed was that the city, which seemed so vibrant and colorful at 2am, was back to it's grey, dreary norm by 9. He almost smiled. This was what he remembered. Philly is a tough, no-nonsense type of town and if today was going to be his last time here, he wanted to remember it like this, not some wannabe Manhattan teeming with fake hipsters and clueless tourists. Yes, this felt right.

"You awake?" asked Amber, interrupting his thoughts. "I'm gonna go put in thirty on the treadmill."

"You have to be the only person in the world who showers before going to the gym."

"I don't know about that." she smiled, sitting down on the edge of their king sized bed to put on her running shoes.

He looked away from the window and focused on his wife. It amazed him how, after almost seven years, she could still take his breath away. She was truly the most beautiful woman he had ever seen and, right now, he wanted nothing more than to be close to her.

"Sorry about last night." he said as he got up out of his chair and laid down on the bed.

"For what? Being human?" she asked with a smile. "Babe, you buried your mother yesterday, it's perfectly natural for you to show some emotion. Honestly I would've been worried if you didn't."

"Yea, but the whole thing had to be kinda weird for you."

"Why?" she interrupted. "Because I never met your mother or anyone else in your family before yesterday?"

He flopped his head down on the bed and stared up at the ceiling. He knew she was right, of course, but didn't know what to say. There were so many things she didn't know...so many things she couldn't know.

"Listen," she said, moving closer to him. "You made it perfectly clear when we met that your past was not something you wanted to deal with and I have always respected that."

"And now?"

"Mark, I have never pushed you to tell me anything about your family, but I am your wife and I do love you so at some point; And I'm not saying right now or tomorrow or even next week, but at some point I think we need to at least have a conversation about where you come from."

"The past is the past Amber." he replied quietly, shutting down as he always did whenever this topic came up.

"And sometimes the past can effect the future..." she pushed back.

"I don't see how."

She knew she needed to tell him why she was pushing, but ultimately decided it wasn't the right time. "Listen, we can talk about this more later." she said reassuringly. He'd been through enough for right now and it's not like they wouldn't have plenty of time to talk about this, or anything else, later. She leaned over and gave him a soft kiss. "Why don't you try and get some sleep. I'll be downstairs in the gym."

After she left he laid there, staring at the ceiling until his mind was made up. For a brief moment this morning he thought about skipping tonight but, after listening to his wife, he realized she was right. He couldn't keep running from his past forever. Sooner or later he would have to deal with what he left behind and now, with his mother gone, he felt like he was ready to do exactly that. He reached for his phone.

Sep 11, 2013 9:45 AM

u get tickets?

Ur supposed 2

be sleep :)

trying

u get em?

Ya.

u still wanna

go 2nite?

yep

Y? ur not

into dance

mom was

kinda makes me

21

feel close 2 her

can go solo

if u want?

Hello??

not a chance mister

now go 2 sleep!

He figured it was worth a shot. He always planned for Amber to be with him but knew this would be much easier if she wasn't. The last thing in the world he could afford was for his wife to find out what he was hiding. As much as he was sure she loved him, he knew there were certain things she could never accept. Fortunately, as long as everything went as planned, she would never have to...

CHAPTER THREE

When Walter finally came out of the bathroom, Lisa was busy on her laptop trying to get some work done. He'd been in the shower for twenty minutes and, as usual, was taking nearly twice as long to get ready as she did. Oh well, she smiled to herself, the end result was usually pretty impressive.

When he made his way past her wearing nothing but a towel, she knew he was trying to get her attention. She glanced up only long enough to point to the wall clock, reminding him they were running late.

"If you wanna go ahead, I can just meet you down there." he shouted from the bedroom as she closed her computer and put away her work. "I'd hate to make you late."

Lisa just smiled without responding; after five years, she had learned to take Walter's sarcasm in stride. She waited another ten minutes before he came out of the bedroom dressed casually in a pair of jeans and a loose fitting white shirt, his go-to outfit when he wanted to look like he didn't care what he was wearing. She also noticed he had on her favorite jeans, his not so subtle way of saying he expected to be rewarded for sacrificing his Friday night.

"Do I really have to go to this thing?" he asked, putting on his jacket. "I haven't even had dinner."

"Stop whining." she replied, grabbing her purse and coat, "you could use a little culture."

"Culture?" he asked, looking at her as if she'd lost her mind. "Lisa c'mon, they're high school kids."

"And you're a grown man who wants to get laid tonight." she finished his thought with a smile. "You have the tickets?"

She had him and they both knew it. He was standing in the mirror, doing a final wardrobe check, before reaching into his jacket pocket and pulling out a white envelope.

Satisfied her point was made, she walked behind him, snatched the tickets out of his hand and playfully squeezed his butt. "Now hurry up." she said as she made her way toward the front door. "I don't want to be late."

The twenty minute ride into the city went smoothly and they walked into the lobby about five minutes before show time. Most of the audience had already made their way into the theater save for a few stragglers standing by two make-shift concession tables. He counted six people in total, two attendants, two people being waited on and two people in line waiting.

"Perfect." he said, stopping in line behind the two remaining customers. "You want anything?"

"Just hurry up." said Lisa as she casually flipped through the program. "I don't want to miss the opening piece."

The Annenberg Center for the Performing Arts is located downtown on the University of Pennsylvania campus. Long considered to be one of the premier performance venues in Philadelphia, it made perfect sense that a special tribute on the eleven year anniversary of 9/11 was being held there. What didn't make sense was why her husband was so determined to see it.

For a second, she almost believed the thing about feeling closer to his mother, a woman he hadn't seen or spoken to for at least five years. That is until she remembered him asking about the tickets the week before she died. At the time he said they were for a client so she didn't think anything of it. Now, with everything he'd been through, he obviously didn't realize his story had changed…

Amber Stafford-O'Connor didn't like being lied to, but she HATED feeling manipulated. The night before, her heart ached for him as he cried himself to sleep in her arms. She felt as close to him as ever and fell asleep feeling safer and more secure in their relationship than she thought possible. Yet by the next morning, less than five hours later, he felt it was ok to disrespect her? Not only that, the lying sonofabitch had the audacity to use the death of his mother to cover whatever he was hiding.

As far as she knew, Mark had never lied to her before and she was going to make damn sure he knew it better not happen again. Apparently her husband had lost his mind along with his mother and she was going to take great pleasure in putting him back in his place. First she was determined to find out what he was so desperately trying to keep from her.

As the cab pulled up in front of the theater, Amber still had no idea why they were there or, more importantly, what she was about to walk into. Whatever it was, it couldn't be good if he went through the trouble of telling not one but TWO lies to hide it.

Mark was completely lost in his own world. Under normal circumstances he would have probably noticed his wife hadn't said a word to him since they left the hotel, but this situation was far from normal. He kept telling himself it would all be over soon. He just had to make it to intermission, excuse himself to use the restroom and make his way backstage. The whole thing would take less than ten minutes and then he would be free to move on with his life.

They entered the lobby right as the house lights were being brought down to half, the universal signal of a show about to begin. His heart was racing with anticipation as they picked up their programs and made their way toward the ushers manning the theater entrance. As much as he tried to act normal, he was a nervous wreck inside.

He noticed his mouth starting to feel excessively dry so, when he saw the concession table by the entrance, he stopped to grab some candy.

"Can I get a pack of lifesavers?"

"Excuse me," said Walter from behind them. "We were next in line."

Startled, Mark turned to see Walter and Lisa standing about two feet behind him. He noticed they were holding hands and, without responding, shot Amber a quick look, shook his head and turned back to the attendant standing behind the table.

"How much are these?" he asked matter of factly.

Walter looked at Lisa in disbelief. He let go of her hand and took a step forward toward Mark and Amber. "We were next." he said assertively.

Mark didn't turn this time, purposely ignoring what was happening behind him as he reached into his jacket pocket for his wallet.

"Are you deaf?" asked Walter, moving closer.

"There are two lines dude." said Amber dismissively as she positioned herself between the two men. "Pick one."

Walter couldn't help but notice how attractive she was and this kind of disarmed him. She was standing close enough for him to recognize the scent of her Caron's Poivre perfume and see that she was wearing a pair of Jimmy Choo mesh pumps.

These two definitely had money and while he knew sometimes people with money acted like asses, this was insane. The woman was literally less than half his size. Even in her four and three quarter inch heels, she barely came up to his chest. Yet she stood in front of him as if she knew he couldn't do anything about it. "I aint your dude alright." he replied, trying to remain as calm as possible.

Amber stood her ground, not the least bit intimidated by his size and wanting him to know it. Sensing things were about to get out of hand, Lisa stepped forward and gently grabbed Walter by the wrist.

"Babe, let it go." she said not wanting things to escalate. "let's just go over to the other server." It worked, almost, until Walter noticed the smirk on Ambers face as he started to move toward the other end of the concession table.

"You know what, damn that." he said as he yanked his arm free of Lisa's grasp and moved past Amber to get into Mark's face. "The line starts behind us."

Amber quickly grabbed Mark by the shoulder, pulled him back and repositioned herself between him and Walter. She looked over at Lisa who was now firmly grabbing Walter's arm, trying to pull him back, away from the situation. She waited until they had made solid eye contact before speaking.

"Can you control your *pet* please?"

CHAPTER FOUR

He was sure he must have heard her wrong. That is until he looked over and saw the expression on Lisa's face confirming he had, in fact, heard exactly what this bitch just said.

He'd experienced ignorance before, but nothing quite like this. He was a pretty big guy, after all, so even if they thought it, the average person would usually think twice before saying it out loud in front of him.

These two were different. They were like the kind of over the top characters you might see in a movie about some small town in the south. Only this wasn't a movie and this damn sure wasn't Alabama, or Georgia, or wherever the hell else these two thought they were. Without thinking about it any further, he started removing his jacket, drawing a sarcastic laugh from Amber.

"You think this shit is funny?"

"Whatever, tough guy." she answered with a confidence that completely belied her petite frame.

The girls working the concession table, who couldn't have been more than fifteen or sixteen, looked helplessly at each other, not quite knowing what to do or say.

"Jenny, go and get Mr. C." said one of them nervously.

"What?"

"Go and get Mr. Cohen! Hurry up."

Hearing this, Mark realized immediately this was neither the time nor the place to be dealing with this. "Look man," he said to Walter from behind his wife. "We're sorry ok? We just wanted to get to our seats." He took Amber's hand and started walking toward the entrance. She, reluctantly, turned to join her husband.

"Apologize." said Walter, angrily, as soon as Amber's back was to him.

"I just said we were sorry. What more do you..."

"Her." Walter interrupted, pointing at Amber. "Your girl needs to apologize or we are gonna have a problem."

"Baby just let it go, ok." said Lisa softly. "They aren't worth it."

Mark couldn't help but shake his head at seeing the two of them together. There was plenty he wanted to say but he reminded himself that now wasn't the time. "This conversation is over." he said firmly, turning to walk away for the final time.

Walter had no intention of letting anything go. He dropped his jacket, snatched his arm away from Lisa, causing her to stumble backwards, and took a step toward Mark. He was just about in reach when Amber, in one fluid motion, dropped her bag, let go of Mark's hand and spun around to her left. Walter's eyes followed and quickly focused on her right hand, where what was once a nine hundred dollar Marc Jacobs handbag was now a nine millimeter semi-automatic handgun aimed squarely into his chest. He instinctively took a step back and slowly raised his hands to his sides, making sure to avoid any sudden movement that might spook this crazy bitch into doing something they would all regret, him more than anyone.

This wasn't his first time seeing a gun nor was it the first time he had one pointed in his direction. He knew not to panic and that he had to, somehow, de-escalate the situation. That wouldn't be easy.

There was something in this chicks eyes that sent a chill through him. There was none of the blind rage or nervous energy that normally accompanied these situations. She was calm; too calm. Almost like a deer hunter with a large buck in her sights. He sensed she would not hesitate to squeeze the trigger if she had to so he kept moving backwards, trying to create enough distance between them that she might relax and lower the gun. Slowly and steadily he made his way across the lobby, but his plan didn't seem to be working. He was almost to the door but not only was she not lowering her weapon, her eyes seemed more fixated on him than before. It was almost as if she was looking through him. Like there was something behind...

It was too late when he noticed her eyes dart quickly to his right. He never saw the seven men in black hoodies entering the lobby behind him and was tackled hard to the ground before he could react. They were on him so quickly he barely put up a fight as they covered his head with some kind of canvas bag, descending his world into complete darkness. The next thing he felt was a large, serrated knife being pressed hard against the back of his neck, making it impossible for him to move. Blind and unable to respond he could only listen helplessly to muted screams and what he thought had to be gun fire coming from inside the theatre.

Amber had immediately noticed the men congregating outside the lobby doors behind her target, but had become so fixated on them she was a split second late recognizing the second group entering through the doors to her left. "Mark look out!" she screamed, too late, as one of the men jumped her husband, knocking him to the ground. Showing no hesitation, she pivoted to her left and squeezed her trigger in their direction, dropping two of the assailants before a third returned fire, missing wide but hitting the teenage girl working behind the concession table in the chest, showering

Amber in her blood and distracting her just long enough that a fourth man could launch himself into her ribs, knocking the gun from her hands and sending her screaming and crashing violently onto the table. The impact to her mid-section left her gasping for air as the man who tackled her maneuvered his way on top and punched her hard in the face, nearly knocking her unconscious. He then grabbed her by the hair, threw her to the ground and covered her head.

And just like that, it was over. The lobby was eerily silent as Mark, Lisa, Amber and Walter were held, face down, on the ground with their heads covered. Unable to see what was going on, all they could do was lie still, wait, and pray. The foul stench of pooling blood would have probably been nauseating under normal circumstances, but they were still too much in shock to notice. The adrenaline of the initial assault had begun to dissipate however and fear was beginning to set in. Almost in synch, each of them started to physically shake as the reality of their situation began to take hold. Just as they were about to reach a full on panic, their assailants sprung back into action, grabbing each of them by the hair, careful not to remove their hoods, and pulling them to their feet. Walter, Lisa and Mark each had a sharp knife held firmly against their throats while Amber, as a reward for her earlier heroics, received the special honor of several hard punches to her already cracked ribs. She doubled over and shrieked in pain from each of the blows, causing Mark to flinch just enough to get the attention of his attacker who knocked him back to the ground with a hard kick to the back of his left knee.

A second later, they were all back on their feet, being led down some steps and through a narrow hallway. After a short walk down a few more flights of steps, a door was opened and they were ushered, unceremoniously, into a cold, damp room and pushed back to the ground. This time though, their attackers didn't forcefully hold them down. In fact, almost immediately after they were thrown on the floor, they heard the door shut and the room fell silent. None of them dared move, much less try and remove the bags from their heads. They were content to sit still and wait to be told what to do next. They would be waiting a long time.

If any of them had been thinking straight, they would have probably noticed that throughout this entire ordeal, from the fire fight in the lobby to the assault on the theater, and the walk to where ever they were being held now, throughout all of this, none of the men now holding them hostage had uttered a single word...

CHAPTER FIVE

Amber's head felt heavy. She had apparently dozed off only to be awakened by a deep throbbing emanating from the small of her back, up through her spine and into her neck. She slowly opened her eyes but remained immersed in darkness because of the bag still placed haphazardly on her head. She felt her pulse quicken as the reality of where she was and how she got there slowly came back.

"Mark?" she said in a whisper that was only slightly audible. No response.

She re-closed her eyes and focused on listening to what was going on around her. She could definitely hear breathing, so she knew she wasn't alone. The problem was she had no way of knowing who else was there.

Nobody was talking or moving so there was, at least, a possibility they were locked in the room by themselves. There was just no way to know for sure.

What she did know was this concrete floor was freezing cold and she desperately needed to try and get up.

She made it a point to move very deliberately. As much as she might have hoped they were alone, their attackers could just as easily have been sitting two feet away with automatic weapons pointed at their heads. Knowing this, she knew better than to make any kind of sudden movement.

Listening closely for any reaction or movement in her direction, she slowly tried to get to her hands and knees but was stopped by a sharp, piercing pain in her side.

"Are you ok?"

It was a man's voice and it was nearby. The pain in her side persisted, making it difficult to focus, but judging from the tone of the voice, he was older and saw himself as some sort of authority figure. She gingerly shifted her weight onto her knees and braced herself for a reaction. When nothing happened, she slowly reached for the bag still covering her head.

"Here let me help you." the man said softly as he helped her remove it.

She opened her eyes and immediately tried to scan her surroundings, blinking hard as her eyes took a few seconds to adjust to the low level of light in the room. She could see well enough to recognize her husband lying face down on the floor less than three feet in front of her.

"Mark!" she hurried over next to him. "Wake up baby! Are you ok?!"

He'd been knocked unconscious when his head hit the floor so it took him a minute to clear the cobwebs and remember where they were. He felt nauseous, and more than a little dizzy, so he sat himself up slowly as Amber removed the bag from his head.

"Oh thank god you're ok." she said, tossing the bag aside and lunging into his arms. "I was so scared something happened to you."

He wrapped his arms around her waist and held her close, not so much to reassure her as to prevent her from seeing the terrified look in his eyes. She buried her head in his chest and began sobbing uncontrollably which only made his feelings of helplessness worse. It was supposed to be his job to protect her and yet, when the shooting started, it was his wife standing her ground against the bad guys while he was being knocked to the floor. It didn't matter that his father in-law owned four of the five largest shooting ranges in the country or that his wife had practically been born with a gun in her hand. The natural order of things mandated his role as the protector, not the protected, and he had failed miserably. Not to mention, neither of them would have been there in the first place had it not been for him and his bullshit. He had to get them out of this. He would never forgive himself if anything happened to her tonight.

As he stroked Amber's hair and reassured her that everything would be fine, he looked around the room and noticed, for the first time, that they weren't alone. He counted seven people including their 'friends' from the concession stand earlier. He quickly looked down at the ground to avoid making eye contact with anyone and focused all of his attention on calming his wife.

Lisa and Walter had already removed the bags from their heads and were sitting quietly in a corner by themselves. Physically they were both fine but still horribly shaken by what happened in the lobby. Lisa, in particular, was having a very difficult time dealing with it. Unlike Amber however, she was working really hard not to show any overt signs of panic in front of their fellow hostages, two of whom were young kids.

When she saw there were children in the room, her teachers instincts kicked in and she knew to keep her emotions in check, at least as best she could. Experience taught her that if the adults panicked, the kids would follow suit and that wouldn't be good for anyone.

"What do you think?" she asked Walter nervously, hoping to find some measure of comfort in the sound of his voice.

"Just sit tight and do what they say. We'll be ok."

Far from comforting, his words rang hollow, not that she could blame him. The fact of the matter was, there wasn't a damn thing anyone could have said to make her feel better. In fact, the only measure of comfort she could draw from their current state of affairs was that they were both still breathing which, to be honest, was no small feat. They had both been in the lobby where an innocent teenage girl was gunned down, in cold blood, by the same animals who locked them in this room. The realization that their fate was now in the hands of a group of cold blooded killers did not leave much room for reassurance. Quite the opposite, it made it that much more difficult to hide how afraid she really was.

She looked around the room and wondered what everyone else might be thinking. They had all instinctively carved out a piece of real estate for themselves and huddled closely with their significant others, silently waiting for something to happen.

All except for the tough looking older gentleman sitting close to the door who, of everyone, appeared to be the handling the situation the best. He was sitting by himself but Lisa had the distinct impression this was by choice. He projected a sense of calm which gave her the feeling he was in charge in some way. She started focusing more of her attention on him than the others.

No one was saying or doing anything and since the silence was starting to get to her, she decided to try and break the ice.

"Any idea what's going on?"

"What the hell do you think is going on?" Mark snapped.

"I wasn't talking to you."

"Look, the rag heads said to sit here and shut up, so you need to sit there and shut the fuck up!"

"Yo!" shouted Walter, waiting until he was sure he had the little guy's full attention before going on, "Who the hell do you think you're talking to?"

"She's gonna get us killed man!"

Mark's voice was trembling with fear but Walter couldn't have cared less. The way he saw it, this asshole didn't deserve any compassion after the way he and his girl acted in the lobby. Between that and this little outburst right now, Walter had heard more than enough from this idiot for one night. The next ignorant thing out of his mouth and he was going to get up and personally beat some respect into him.

"Let it go."

It was the guy sitting by the door. Walter looked over to see who he was talking to and, sure enough, the man was looking directly at him. Before he could tell the old guy to mind his business, he stood up from his seat and extended his hand in Walter's direction.

"Robert" he said, calmly introducing himself.

Walter looked him up and down for a long moment before grudgingly accepting his handshake.

"Walter"

"Nice to meet you." smiled Robert, sitting down in front of Walter, purposely placing himself between the two rivals. He looked over at Lisa and extended his hand again. "And you?"

"Lisa Woodward"

"Pleasure…"

"So," said Lisa, desperate to keep the conversation from dying. "Were you a part of the show?"

"No. Well sort of. I'm directing a piece for my school."

"Really? What school…"

"What the fuck?!" Mark snapped again. He was still in a panic but now focused more on Robert than either Walter or Lisa. "Are you retarded or something?! We're being held hostage for christ's sake!"

"And the worst thing we can do is panic." said Robert, calmly.

"No, we should pretend we're in summer camp."

"Calm down." Robert insisted. "If we do what we're told, no one will get hurt."

"What are you?" Mark asked sarcastically. "Some kinda expert?"

"You need to chill out man."

Dexter, a fourteen year old black kid, was there with his sister, Toshia. The two of them, like everyone else, were getting tired of Mark's attitude.

"Nobody's talking to you." replied Mark, angrily. He wasn't about to be disrespected by some punk kid, even if this particular 'kid' was about two inches taller than him.

"Let's all settle down," Robert said forcefully, determined to get control of the situation before things got out of hand. He knew the best chance they had of getting through this was if they kept their emotions in check and used their heads. None of that would be possible if he couldn't keep them from trying to kill each other.

As a former marine, dealing with stress was nothing new to him, only he wasn't worried about himself. Right now, his biggest challenge was going to be keeping the other so-called grown ups from melting down completely, at least long enough for him to figure out what the hell was going on. Unfortunately, judging by the last few minutes, they weren't going to make that very easy.

Everyone sat silently for a few minutes, almost as if they were trying to re-set their emotions and start over. None of them knew exactly what to make of their situation or, more importantly, what they should try and do about it. Lacking any kind of direction or plan, they just sat there, not doing or saying anything.

The quiet was not sitting well with Lisa. Every minute they sat in silence, her mind inched back closer toward the memory of what happened in the lobby and the image of that girl, lying on the floor, bleeding to death. Remembering her last, desperate gasps for air while those animals stepped over her body as if it was some sort of oversized road-kill was too much for Lisa to take. She thought about the girls parents and shuddered at what they would be going through when they found out they would have to bury their child. How would anyone explain to them why they would never see their little girl again?

Most of all, she would have to come to grips with the fact that she stood less than three feet away and had done nothing to stop it. A family was torn apart right before her eyes and the only thing she would be able to offer them was a series of meaningless platitudes that, in the end, would do nothing to either ease their pain or lessen the burden of truth she would be carrying with her for the rest of her life. And that truth was that while their baby girl lied on a cold floor fighting for her last breath, the only thing she did was lie next to her, watching her die.

The deathlike silence in the room was growing louder by the second and she felt herself physically beginning to shake. If she was going to have any chance of holding herself together, she had to stop thinking about what happened in the lobby. That much was clear. She looked around the room for something, anything, to focus her attention on but found nothing useful. The walls were completely bare and the room was filled mainly with old furniture and random set pieces, not exactly thought provoking decor.

"Hey," she blurted out awkwardly, her voice still shaking. "Sorry about before, I was just trying to make conversation." The fact that she got through the sentence without vomiting struck her as something close to a miracle. Only no one responded, so she decided to push on. "I just figured..."

"Oh my god!" shouted Mark in frustration. The quiet had been fine with him. In fact, he was perfectly willing to sit there in complete silence until this whole nightmare was over. He looked around the room and saw that all eyes were now on him. "Ok fine. You guys wanna go around the room? Ok then," he stood up to make his point. "Hi everyone my name is Mark..."

"...And I'm a fucking idiot." Dex chimed in, finishing his sentence and getting a slight smirk from Walter. Seeing the two of them laugh at his expense irritated Mark even more and made him want to lash out aggressively.

"Oh yea," he said, looking directly at Dex. "Well, why don't you try and spell it sambo."

Being so young, the meaning of the word was lost on Dex. The implication of disrespect, however, was very clear. Walter, on the other hand, knew exactly what the word meant and shot Lisa a quick look of disbelief. This little guy had balls, he had to give him that much.

"Don't get your ass kicked homey." Dex replied, standing up quickly. He was bigger than this little dude and wanted him to know it.

"You say so?" Mark responded, determined not to back down.

"Yeah I say so." replied Dex, taking a step toward him.

"Mark stop it."

Amber had heard enough. The pain in her side wasn't getting any better and this was neither the time or the place for her husband to be trying to prove his manhood.

Toshia had heard enough as well and quickly jumped to her feet to restrain her little brother. "Dexter, sit your ass down."

He complied without protest, taking a seat on an old sofa against the far wall. He was still pissed however so he wasn't about to let it go.

"What's your problem anyway?" he asked, from across the room.

"Aint it obvious?" Mark replied, almost under his breath.

"Why don't you enlighten us?" asked Walter, basically daring him to say the wrong thing. At this point, he was looking for an excuse to shut this clown up himself.

"Whatever man," Mark replied without looking up. "Just don't get too close."

"Afraid you might get infected?" Walter persisted.

"He probably thinks it'll rub off or something." Dex offered, earning an approving nod and wink from Walter.

Amber's head was still throbbing with pain and she, like her husband, wanted everyone to sit quietly until this was all over. "Just leave us alone ok?" she pleaded, almost innocently.

Dex wasn't having any of it. "Wait a minute." he said quickly, addressing Amber. "Wasn't nobody thinkin bout his little bitch ass til he started tellin everybody to shut the fuck…"

"AHEM!!"

The voice seemed to catch everyone off guard. Eleodora and her fifteen year old daughter, Lena, had been sitting so quietly that the others had honestly forgotten they were even in the room.

"Young man, there are ladies present." she scolded Dex gently.

"Hey look," he whined defensively. "homeboy started it. I was just…"

"Please."

It was clear she knew how to handle children and as loud and cocky as he could be, Dexter was still exactly that.

He got the message and settled down into his seat. As the room went silent yet again, he leaned back into the sofa and closed his eyes. A few seconds later, Toshia came over, put her arm around his shoulder and sat down next to him. Knowing

47

she was ok and that they were together gave him a sense of comfort, which was odd considering where they were and how they got there...

He'd been standing in the wings of the stage when he first heard the commotion, but since he couldn't see what was going on he just assumed it was a part of the performance.

"Dexter get back!"

He looked up to see his sister Toshia running across the stage like a crazy person. Seeing the look on her face, he knew not to ask questions and just get the heck out of there as fast as possible. They could talk about what was going on later.

First, they ran for the stage door exit but whoever was doing this had already blocked it off with a big chain and an even bigger dude holding a rifle. Fortunately, the guy never saw them so they quietly backtracked and ducked down in the stairwell.

"Come on!" whispered a male voice from about two feet behind where they were kneeling. Dex looked up to see his drama teacher bounding past them and heading down the stairs. They followed him to the scene shop, figuring that was as good a place as any to hide. It wasn't until they got to the room that Dex realized his classmate Lena and another lady had been right behind them the entire time. He'd been so focused on getting out of there he never even noticed they weren't alone.

Mr. Cohen shut door behind them and tried to lock it, only to find the lock was broken. "Dammit!" he cursed under his breath and then led the four of them to a far corner where they huddled behind some old set pieces. "Dex come here." he commanded as he grabbed one end of an old sofa and started toward the door. Dex followed suit immediately, realizing the plan was to barricade the door. Too late...

The door flew open violently and two armed men stormed into the room.

Robert Cohen wasn't just a retired Marine, he was force-recon, the Marine Corps's elite special operations force. He knew survival in these situations never came down to who was the toughest. In fact, he had learned a long time ago that the idea of physical toughness was a myth. The whole concept probably created by insecure men trying to convince themselves of something they weren't sure of. There was no such thing as 'tough' or 'soft.' There was trained and there was untrained, nothing else.

He was the closest to the door when the two gunmen entered and immediately noticed the first guy holding his weapon too high. The idiot also allowed the barrel to get a little closer to Roberts forehead than he should have. He was probably trying to be intimidating but his tough guy act had actually given Robert an opening if he chose to take it.

The problem was the second guy, who had obviously been better trained than his buddy. He came in the room and, after assessing the situation, quickly fanned out to his left, creating some distance and a clear line-of-sight for himself.

Robert was confident he could easily disarm this first clown but there was no way he'd be able to secure his weapon and deal with the second threat in time to prevent him from getting multiple shots off. He might have been able to protect himself by using the body of the first guy as cover, but there was nothing he could do to protect any of the others and that was unacceptable.

He dropped his end of the sofa, raised his hands and took a small step backward. He didn't want to go too far, in case he had to make a move, but he didn't want to risk spooking the guy holding a gun two inches from his brain either. He composed himself and was about to say something when four more gunmen entered the room, only this time they weren't alone.

Each of them had a partner who dragged a hostage into the room behind them. They had taken the time to cover their heads with some sort of sack, so it was obvious the bad guys knew exactly where they were going and were probably planning on using this room as some sort of holding area all along. "Way to go Mr. C" he admonished himself. "You led your people directly into the enemy prison."

He shook off the thought and re-focused on the task at hand. Out manned and out gunned, his only course of action was to start some sort of dialog. If he could get them talking, he might be able to find who was in charge. He didn't know yet how he would leverage that piece of information but he knew it would be useful. If nothing else, he could find out what they wanted.

"My name is Robert Cohen." he said, allowing his voice to project an audible shake. The more afraid he seemed the less likely they would see him as a threat and THAT would definitely come in handy. "Everyone here will do whatever you say." he continued. "Tell me what you want."

Without responding, the gunmen threw their four hostages onto the floor, and began filing out of the room. When the original two were the only ones left, the second guy slowly walked toward where Robert was still being held at gunpoint. His movement in their direction made his partner a little antsy, letting Robert know who was in charge, between these two at least.

When Omer was close enough to whisper, he leaned into Robert's ear so no one else would hear what he had to say.

"You will know what we want soon enough."

CHAPTER SIX

Dex noticed his feet getting cold, which was odd seeing as it was only September. It'd been a little cooler than normal this year but it wasn't exactly freezing and besides, he usually loved the cold. He and Toshia fought all the time about him falling asleep with the windows open in the middle of the winter.

"Boy, I'm not paying to heat the porch!" she would scream from the living room. "Shut that damn window!"

"But it's hot in here and I can't sleep."

"Then just lie there until school tomorrow. I bet you'll fall asleep eventually."

They had the argument so many times, he could recite it from memory. He looked over at his big sister, who was leaning back on the sofa next to him, eyes closed, arms folded tightly across her chest. He couldn't tell if she was sleeping or not but figured she had to be freezing. The scene shop was in the basement, so it was a cold, damp type of place to begin with. This would have been bad enough but, like most girls, Toshia was ALWAYS cold. It could be 70 degrees outside and this crazy chick would have a sweater on.

He looked around and noticed an old blanket on the floor in front of them. It was dirty and he had no idea how long it'd been sitting there but it was definitely better than nothing. He picked it up, covered Toshia with it and then settled back into the sofa next to her.

Fortunately, the blanket was large enough to cover his feet too, so he solved both of his problems with one solution. Well, technically he had more than 'two' problems at the moment. Whatever; At least now he didn't have to worry about his feet freezing off. Now only if he could find something to eat.

He had just gotten comfortable when it occurred to him he was hungry. He didn't know exactly how long they'd been locked up but he knew he hadn't eaten in a while and his stomach was growling. A quick glance around the room and it was obvious he wasn't going to find any food lying on the floor in front of them. At least nothing he could eat.

"Whatever," he thought to himself. "I'll deal."

The initial shock of everything started to wear off and he was beginning to feel a little antsy. Without thinking, he stood up from the couch to stretch his legs and, even though everyone else in the room was sitting perfectly still, his movement didn't seem to elicit any kind of response. They just sat there like zombies.

He was about to say something to Toshia but remembered she was sleeping. When he looked over at her, he noticed she had barely moved herself for at least the past hour, which made him uneasy. He looked back at the others and noticed they were awake, but sitting there with blank expressions on their faces. The whole scene was starting to seriously freak him out. He wasn't used to sitting still for such long periods of time and he certainly wasn't accustomed to being this quiet.

"Hey Miss Gonzalez," he said to Lena, determined to get some kind of conversation going. "You ok over there?"

"I'm fine." she replied softly, her voice barely above a whisper.

"So, is this your moms?" he asked.

"Where's captain obvious when you need him?"

The smart ass remark came from Mark, of course, but that was actually a good thing. Dex had a lot of nervous energy and needed something to focus it on. Who better than Mr. Sunshine?

"Why don't you 'captain' my nuts?"

"Dexter!"

Toshia apparently wasn't asleep after all.

"Sorry." he apologized quickly, acknowledging the look on her face telling him she wasn't playing.

Relieved he had actually woken up the room , he wasn't about to let the energy die out again. He walked away from the couch over to the corner where Lena and her mother were sitting.

"Hello ma'am." he said smoothly as he extended his hand to Eleodora. "My name is Dexter Swindell. Everybody calls me Dex."

"Hello Dexter." she replied quickly, shaking his hand. "I am Lena's mother, Mrs. Gonzalez."

"Nice to meet you, and let me say that you have a lovely daughter."

"Dex." This time it was Mr. C. trying to rain on his parade.

"Hey, I'm just trying to be polite." he replied mischievously, flashing his best smile.

"This isn't a game."

"You said don't panic right? And besides if they wanted us dead we'd be blowed up by now."

"You an expert too?" asked Toshia.

"Don't take no Einstein to figure that out Tosh."

"Regardless," Robert said firmly. "This is serious. Now sit tight and do what you're told."

"Alright Mr. C. I'll chill."

He sat back down next to Toshia but immediately after he took his seat, the awkward silence began creeping it's way back into the room. They all quickly realized how much they'd welcomed Dexter's little distraction.

"Any idea what they want?" asked Toshia, nervously trying to keep some kind of conversation going.

"God only knows what they want." Walter answered abruptly, getting a nervous reaction from the others. "Look," he continued, immediately realizing his error. "Dex is probably right. If they wanted us dead we wouldn't be here right now."

"I guess we have 3 experts in the house." Mark replied under his breath, barely loud enough to be heard.

"You need to freeze the attitude dawg. For real."

"They told you to be quiet!" Amber exploded. She was beginning to HATE the sound of this kids voice. "Do you not understand what that means?!"

"Why don't you tell me what it means." Dex shot back defiantly.

"Sorry bro, we don't speak Ebonics."

The last comment came from Mark. Hearing it, Walter decided he was through putting up with this asshole. He stood up but Lisa quickly grabbed him around the waist and pulled him back.

"Would you guys stop?!" she shouted in frustration and positioned herself between the two of them. "Like it or not we are in here together so everybody just needs to get over it!"

"I'll bet you like it."

"Excuse me?"

Lisa was looking directly at Amber whose last comment apparently came out a little louder than she had intended. Neither Amber or Mark bothered responding.

"Don't be no punk now!" Dexter chimed in loudly. "Say what you feel girl."

"Stop instigating." Toshia scolded him half-heartedly. She too was getting tired of these two.

"Hey look," he smiled. "I'm just trying to make the best of a bad situation."

"Just be quiet."

"Don't get mad at me. Aint my fault we got kidnapped and stuck in a room with some wannabe skinheads."

"Well, you seem relaxed." Lisa suggested, trying to change the subject but desperately wanting to keep the conversation going.

"I'm too sexy to be a hostage."

"Boy, shut up." Toshia laughed, rolling her eyes.

The comment caught Lisa off guard and forced a genuine a smile. She was starting to really like this kid.

"You guys friends?"

"He's my little brother." Toshia answered, playfully pushing him in the side of his head.

"Good looking family huh?" Dex said proudly. "Go on, you can say it."

"Hi. I'm Toshia."

Lisa took her hand and smiled warmly, happy to be enjoying a civil conversation. "Lisa. And this is my boyfriend Walter." she replied, gesturing in Walter's direction.

"Okay!" exclaimed Dexter, jumping off the sofa and rushing over to Walter who was standing behind Lisa. "I see you big man! Now I like the sisters myself. And of course I love my latin mommies. But she doin it. She got a lil somethin somethin."

"Thank you Dexter." Lisa laughed.

"Umm, everybody calls me Dex."

"Oh, I see." she responded playfully. "Then thank you Dex."

Lisa looked around the room and took a deep breath. She was surprisingly starting to feel somewhat ok about the situation. At least as ok as she could be under the circumstances. She, like the others, had lost track of how much time they'd been in the room but it was long enough that she started to think maybe they'd been forgotten. Or that's what she tried telling herself.

She looked over at Mark and Amber, who were going out of their way to separate themselves from the rest of the group, and couldn't help but notice how attractive, and thin, Amber was. This made it that much easier to dislike her, not that she needed any more reason after some of the vile things that had come out of her mouth.

None of that mattered now, Lisa corrected herself. They were all in this room together and none of them would be going anywhere anytime soon. It would definitely be better to suck it up and make the best of it than to constantly be at each others throats. Mark and Amber were still huddling together quietly when Lisa decided to try and make peace with them. If nothing else, it would keep the conversation going and make her feel like she was the bigger person, in more than just the negative sense.

"Hi." she said, offering her hand to Amber, who looked up and winced in pain as she tried to turn away.

"Are you ok?" she asked, genuinely concerned and placing a hand on Amber's back.

"Don't touch me." Amber rebuked her sharply as Mark knocked her hand off his wife's back.

"What is wrong with you?"

"I don't touch traitors." Amber replied quickly.

"Traitors?"

"Just leave her alone alright?" Mark commanded. He could see Amber was hurting and it killed him that he couldn't do anything to help. The one thing he could do was keep these freaks from harassing her and so he was determined to do exactly that.

Dex, who had been watching the whole time, couldn't help but laugh. "Man, y'all come straight out of a comic book."

"Like you could even read one." Mark shot back angrily.

"Wait a minute." Lisa interrupted, not wanting to get sidetracked. "Why am I a traitor?"

"Just shut up and leave us alone alright!" Amber demanded, her voice shaking.

"If you have something to say, then you should say it."

"You're not worth my time sweetie." Amber replied with a purposely fake smile.

"My name is Lisa."

"Whatever. Just go away."

Lisa was not the violent type and would never condone hitting someone in anything other than self defense, but it was literally all she could do not to smack that smug, fake smile off this cute little bitches face.

"I'm not the one who has us locked up in here you know." she said, turning to walk away before she did something she might regret.

"Yeah I know." Amber answered sarcastically. "None of this is your fault."

"What the hell is that supposed to mean?"

"You know exactly what I'm talking about."

"No, I'm afraid I don't."

"Then I feel even more sorry for you."

Amber was done with this conversation. She turned away, determined not to respond to anything else this annoying tramp had to say.

"Well instead of feeling sorry, why don't you educate me?" Lisa asked smugly. A little too smug for Amber to ignore.

"Don't you dare patronize me."

"I'm not." Lisa responded quickly, feigning innocence and putting on a fake smile of her own. "I'm asking you to show me the err of my ways."

"Why can't you just shut up?!" Mark asked, almost pleadingly. He wanted Amber to rest, but that couldn't happen as long as this pig kept bothering her. There was anger building up in him and he wasn't sure he was going to be able to control it. Nor did he know for sure that he wanted to. He had been forced to sit back and watch while those animals attacked and beat his wife and now this one refused to leave her alone. There was only so much he could take. The guys in the lobby had guns, he reminded himself. This bitch just had a big mouth…

"Why don't we all settle down and focus on getting out of here alive."

Robert had been quietly watching the whole discussion progress and sensed things were about to get out of hand. Mark's face was turning red and, having seen that look before, he thought he might be about to do something stupid. He wanted to calm the situation down before things went too far.

"Right." offered Amber sarcastically. "We'll all settle down so that she can go back to betraying her race in peace."

"So we're locked up in here because I'm dating a black man?"

"You don't get it do you?" Amber replied as she struggled to her feet. She learned through the years that a huge part of the problem was good people sitting silently while people like this betrayed them whenever they felt like it. If more good people had the courage to speak up, she thought, maybe idiots like this would have wised up and got the message a long time ago. Well, regardless of how much it hurt, she wasn't about to sit quietly anymore.

"It's people like you that have helped this country turn it's back on god, and now the rest of us are all left to deal with the consequences."

"People like me?"

"Liberals…apologists…race traitors," Amber said, slowly moving closer until she was standing directly in front of Lisa. "People like you."

It was her tone of voice as much as anything. Lisa had heard hateful things many times in her life, especially since she started seeing Walter, but this was something different. The words had a conviction to them that sent a chill up her spine.

"You're ridiculous." she responded weakly.

"No, I'm white." Amber corrected immediately. "And so are you in case you've forgotten."

"I know who I am thank you very much."

"Then act like it."

"Act like what?" Lisa asked, not believing what she was hearing. "A racist ass?"

"Hey!" Mark interrupted, jumping in to assist his wife who was clearly in pain. "knowing who you are and being proud of it does not make you a racist."

"Nor is it any justification for hate." Robert offered softly, feeling compelled to say something but not wanting to aggravate the situation any more than it already was.

"Call it what you want." said Amber, her voice strained with pain as she gingerly lowered herself into an old reclining chair near the door. "We're just saying out loud what a lot of other people are saying in private."

"That's cause y'all know if you run that noise by the wrong cat, you'll get a foot broke off in your ass."

"No." said Mark firmly, tiring of Dex's silly bravado. "it's because so many whites have been brainwashed by liberal lies that now we're surrounded by race traitors and infiltrators." he continued, emphasizing his point by staring directly at Dex. "You are not the problem."

"Well then who is?" asked Lisa, knowing fully well what was coming next.

"It's you!" Amber shouted, her frustration only topped by the sharp pain in her side. "The enemy within."

"Oh my god! Can either of you explain to me how it is my fundamental responsibility as a white person to hate all black people?"

"Don't forget the Jews, the spics and the fags." offered Walter from across the room. He had given up on this conversation a while ago and was merely listening for entertainment purposes at this point. These two clowns were beyond ridiculous and not worth any more of his time or energy. He was actually a little embarrassed he had let them get to him so much earlier. People like this needed to be ignored and all he had done by reacting to their ignorance was give them exactly what they wanted.

"We don't hate anyone." Mark replied. "We love our race and our culture."

"And what culture is that exactly?" Walter asked quickly, leaning forward as if he really wanted to hear the answer.

"Forget it man." Mark answered dismissively. "You would never understand anyway."

"I bet I know what homeboys problem is." offered Dex with a mischievous grin. "Aint really but one reason to hate all them people. My man must be sufferin... from a terminal case... of lack-de-bootay!"

"DEXTER!"

Toshia's and Eleodora's rebuke notwithstanding, Dex went on confidently.

"I'm just saying! You can't expect a man to act right if his drawers aint straight."

As much as he didn't want to be seen encouraging boorish behavior, Walter couldn't help but like the kid. He tried to hold it in but ended up laughing loudly. Seeing Walter lose it made it impossible for Robert to stifle a laugh of his own. What the hell, he thought to himself. He could use a good laugh.

"What are you laughing at?"

Robert's smile quickly faded when he looked up to see Mark staring directly at him. He came close to saying something but thought better of it. Now was definitely not the time. Walter noticed the brief exchange between them and thought something seemed odd. He decided to let it go.

Dexter, as always, was tremendously impressed with himself.

"Look," he went on with his lecture. "Why y'all think we got all this killing going on in the world? Niggas aint getting it in on the regular, that's why! I'm telling you; we wouldn't be locked up in this room right now if them niggas over in Iraq was getting they rocks off properly."

"Dexter," Toshia pleaded. "please stop talking."

"Serious business!" he went on, undeterred. "Miss Gonzalez!" he shouted, looking over at Lena. "Why did your peoples come over here?"

"For a better life." Eleodora replied.

"For freedom." offered Lena softly.

"Exactly!" he shouted. "For life, for liberty and for the pursuit of happiness! All that stuff, right?! Well if you really wanna solve some problems, you need to replace life, liberty and the pursuit of happiness with life, liberty and the pursuit of some hot, sweaty relations!"

Toshia shook her head. She knew enough not to get in the way once her little brother got going. Walter couldn't stop laughing. Appropriate or not, he thought the kid was hilarious. Mark wasn't impressed.

"Join the freaking circus why don't you." he said disgustedly from beside Amber's chair.

"What's that?" Lisa asked.

Mark shot her a dirty look and, for a second, thought maybe it would be better to leave well enough alone. Only this tramps attitude and this kids voice were like fingernails on a chalkboard to him and he was finding it impossible to hide his irritation. Looking around the room, he couldn't help but shake his head at how ignorant they all were.

"Monkeys that talk belong in the circus."

"You honestly believe that?" Lisa asked, her disgust transforming into genuine curiosity.

"Look at em." Amber shot back, every bit as disgusted as her husband.

"That aint what your moms said last…"

"Dex wait," Lisa interrupted, not wanting the conversation to get hijacked. "I really want to hear an answer. You think they're animals?"

"Why are you wasting your time?" Walter asked, not believing she was trying to have an intelligent conversation with these two idiots. "They have nothing to say."

"The evidence is right in front of you." Amber responded, pointedly glaring at Walter as she was speaking.

"What evidence?" Lisa asked, pressing for a clear answer.

"How about a white couple gang-raped and murdered by five over-evolved simians for one example?"

"Where'd you hear that?"

"It's true." Mark responded quickly. "Happened in Tennessee a few years back. When you're through crying about Trayvon you might wanna ask yourself why you haven't heard about it."

"Maybe because it never happened?" Dex suggested.

"Maybe because the media doesn't care when my people get attacked and murdered? I dunno, I guess a couple of innocent white people killed by blacks isn't news worthy."

"I ain't buyin it."

"I'd tell you to look it up but you won't find it listed under rap lyrics."

"Keep runnin your mouth."

"Dexter stop." Lisa stepped in, shifting into teacher mode and motioning for Dex to sit back down. She felt like she was getting somewhere and wanted to go further. "So, assuming this is true, you condemn an entire race of people for the actions of a few?"

"It's not the action, it's the impulse." Amber responded, feeling like she might be able to get through to her.

"Impulse?"

"Listen," Amber began thoughtfully. "When a lion attacks an antelope do you fault the Lion?"

"No, of…"

"Of course not." Amber interrupted. "It is only doing what it must to survive. Now if you bring a lion into your home and feed it and care for it, would you honestly expect it to react like a house cat?"

The room fell silent and Amber saw she had everyone's full attention.

"Of course not," she continued. "Because eventually the lion's instincts would kick in and it would react like a wild animal. Any intelligent person understands this…"

"Is there a point anywhere in our future?" Walt interrupted, tiring of hearing her drone on.

"The point is," Amber continued confidently. "That it makes no sense to condemn animals for being animals and talking monkeys are like any other wild animal. IT acts the only way IT knows how."

"Our mistake was bringing them here." Mark chimed in. "We fed them and we cared for them. And because they looked similar and mimicked our mannerisms we were duped into believing they were human. The real problem today is a culture of race traitors who keep turning them loose on the rest of us."

The room was dead silent. Lisa's anger turned curiosity had morphed into intense sadness by the time Mark finished his little speech. It was one thing to read about people like this in books or to see them on a TV screen, but to be faced with them like this literally made her feel sick to her stomach.

Walter had always said she lived her life in a bubble where bad things never happened to good people. Her retort was always that if he allowed himself to become jaded by the past, it would prevent him from seeing all the progress that had actually been made.

Only this wasn't 1969. This was 2013 and these two believed every word of what they were saying, down to their core. She wanted to tell herself this was only two people and that the deranged ideals of two sick, clearly damaged individuals should hardly matter. Unfortunately she knew better.

She knew this kind of conviction was not an accident. It had not been genetically passed down through some sort of racist strain in their bloodline. This kind of conviction had been nurtured over time, through the consistent and zealous confirmation of others. These two had received and reiterated and, ultimately, reinforced these beliefs amongst a community of like-minded individuals for years.

"Wow." she said, almost to herself, as the magnitude of what she was dealing with began to sink in.

"The evidence," Amber concluded, trying to show Lisa some compassion. "is right there if you would just open your eyes."

"And you honestly believe all this?"

"I believe what my eyes see and my ears hear." Mark responded, his conviction clearly showing. "I believe in Jesus Christ as my lord and savior."

"What do you know of Jesus Christ?"

Eleodora had no intention of getting involved in any part of this discussion but hearing him use the lords name was not going to go unchecked.

For his part, Mark was hardly going to be deterred by some illegal immigrant. As far as he was concerned he had the ultimate truth on his side so he stood up confidently ready to defend his faith.

"If my people, which are called by my name, will humble themselves and pray and seek my face and turn from their wicked ways; Then will I hear from heaven, will forgive their sins, and will heal their land…"

"Wait," Eleodora interrupted, appalled at what she was hearing. "You think the words of the bible are words of hate?"

"We pray a message of hope for white, Christian America." Amber answered from her chair. "We pray for the return of the faith of our ancestors."

"Nonsense," responded Eleodora forcefully. "What you speak is not of the bible."

"Actually it is..."

Walter couldn't have been happier stealing all of the attention in the room away from Mr. and Mrs. Klan.

"What?!" exclaimed both Dex and Lisa. He let silence fill the room again to make sure he had their full attention before speaking.

"The faith they preach," he continued. "IS the faith of their ancestors." He had purposely let the two idiots talk themselves in circles without interruption. Now it was his turn.

"Dawg, you been messin wit her too long." Dex concluded, gesturing in Lisa's direction to make his point.

"I disagree with you." offered Eleodora, emphatically shaking her head.

"That's fine, but hear me out." he responded gently. "Their ancestors were slave owners right?"

"And?"

"Well, Christianity was their faith. My ancestors adopted that faith, along with their language, their arrogance and their culture of violence not because of what they believed but because their survival demanded it. The mimicking they talked about, we refer to as assimilation..."

"Then you agree with what they say?"

"On the basis of historical fact, they're mostly accurate." he continued confidently. "Like it or not, Christianity was absolutely the faith of the slave owners who brought my ancestors here."

"Young man," Eleodora replied firmly. "The bible teaches that all men are the same in the eyes of god."

Anyone who'd actually read it for themselves should know that was a huge misconception but that wasn't a fight he wanted to start at the moment.

"Individual interpretations aside," he responded, skillfully sidestepping the issue without completely conceding the point. "This nation was NOT founded on the basis of religious freedom as some like to say. It was conquered by people hell bent on spreading their faith, through violence if necessary. Now, any people willing to commit genocide to spread the word of their god can't possibly be expected to condemn hatred or discrimination when, as far as they're concerned, it's endorsed in their bible. Which, by the way, they see as the literal word of their god."

"Dawg, you done lost your rabbit assed mind."

"Dex, You're missing my point."

"He's not the only one." said Robert.

"All I'm saying," Walt continued. "Is that when it comes to their history and their faith, what they say if factually true, at least from an historical perspective."

"So they're right to hate us?" asked Toshia, still not quite getting where this was going.

"That's the point Toshia, historically they have no reason to hate us. This nation was built through violence and a visceral contempt for anyone who didn't believe as those who founded it did. What's more, they feel their superiority is anointed to them by a god who created them in his very image. How can the simple logic of all men created equal compete with that?" he paused for a second to let his words sink in.

"So what's the bottom line? Their ancestors brought ours here against their will and they did so in accordance with the tenets of their religion and their god. We, in turn, assimilated to their culture of arrogance, greed and violence. This is the culture they built and they are now reaping what they have sowed They are to blame...them and their religion and their god...not us..."

"Dude," interrupted Mark. "If you hate it here so much, why don't you just go back where you freaking came from?!"

"And that's exactly my point little man!" exclaimed Walter dramatically. "Unfortunately for you, because of what your ancestors did in the name of your god...this IS where I come from."

CHAPTER SEVEN

Marla Cruz loved her new dressing room almost as much as she loved her new townhouse. She had everything custom made, from the sofa to the oversized mirror mounted on the wall behind her stylized dressing table. All of the walls were painted pearl white and the room was outfitted with contemporary furnishings in a variety of pastel colors. Some of her new colleagues, most of whom were at least twenty years her senior, thought it was gaudy or even tacky. She could care less what they thought. They were jealous, antiquated relics of a bygone era that wasn't coming back anytime soon. She represented the future of journalism. This was her time.

She slipped into her silk blouse and checked her figure in the full length mirror in her private bathroom. She loved the image staring back at her, especially the way the sleeveless Elie Tahari accented her well developed arms. She thought about going with the blouse by itself but decided against it, figuring tonight wasn't the right time to push the envelope. Her producer had scored two huge guests to comment on the developing crisis at the Annenberg so she had to play this one straight. She made a mental note to put a little something extra in her personal trainers Christmas stocking this year as she put on her Hugo Boss blazer, checked her hair and made her way out of the bathroom.

Looking around, she couldn't help but smile at the fact that she had a dressing room at all, much less a private one with her own bathroom. Not two years ago, she was a struggling pharmaceutical sales rep, living at home with her parents, doing a fashion and society blog in her spare time. Now she was host of the most watched news talk show in the city and, if she played this current crisis right, it would be one of the most watched in the entire country.

But now wasn't the time for reminiscing. This was her first time covering serious news and it just happened to be the biggest story to hit the city in years, probably since 9/11. And she was the one taking the lead in getting that story out to the public. One thing was for sure, she was going to do it her way. She'd waited too long for this opportunity not to. Nobody wanted to see some middle aged white man reading off a teleprompter anymore. The world was depressing enough.

People needed something new and fresh, which is exactly what she was going to give them.

"Ready in five Marla!"

The following is a transcript from "Street-Wise with Marla Cruz," September 11, 2013. This copy may not be in its final form and may be updated.

MARLA CRUZ, host: Now for the latest on the hostage situation at the Annenberg Center theatre. Moments ago local police and the FBI officials were faxed a memo containing what authorities are calling a list of demands. When asked for specifics, police spokesman Leo Hamm declined further comment although he confirmed there was no explicit threat made against the hostages. With us to discuss these horrifying events is renowned terrorism expert and best selling author Charles Wynn as well as former FBI hostage negotiator Michael Harris. Gentlemen thank you for joining us.

Michael Harris, hostage negotiator: Glad to be here.

Charles Wynn, terrorism expert: Thank you for having us.

Cruz: Charles, first to you. Based on what we've seen and heard so far, what is your assessment of the situation…

Wynn: Well, it's hard to say for sure but it appears these guys are well organized and know exactly what they want to accomplish. Very serious players if you will…

Harris: It's important we keep in mind how little we know. There has been no claim of responsibility and no posturing from the perpetrators, which leads me to agree with Charles. They appear to be disciplined, professional and committed…"

Cruz: Michael, what are the hostages going through right now…What are they feeling?"

Harris: Having been there for a little over an hour, I would imagine they are getting restless. Maybe hungry if they haven't been allowed anything to eat. Whatever the case, I'm certain reality has set in and they are sitting tight hoping for a peaceful resolution.

Wynn: A lot depends on how the perpetrators are handling things inside… With such a large number of people, I'd imagine they are being careful not to insight a panic. That many hostages could very well over run the captors. We all remember the heroic efforts of the passengers of flight 93…It's important for the perpetrators in a situation like this to make sure the hostages have hope…even if it is just an illusion.

Cruz: Charles, how much danger do you think these hostages are in?

Wynn: The lack of any explicit threat concerns me…

Cruz: How so?

Wynn: If an explicit threat were made and tied to a demand, it would give the police a tactical advantage…Knowing the demands would not be met, they'd execute a full breach and save as many hostages as possible before any deadline was reached. Absent that threat or any deadline, the police will be hesitant to risk the hostages …This could allow the perpetrators to begin harming or even killing the hostages without fearing intervention…

Harris: Let me add one more thing…in a building as large as the Annenberg, they could execute one or more hostages inside the building and no one outside the facility would ever know. In fact, if they were to do it in the basement, they could do it without anyone in the theatre knowing…thus avoiding any kind of panic inside.

Cruz: Let's hope that isn't the case… Gentlemen thanks for joining us. Our prayers and best wishes are with the hostages and their families…"

CHAPTER EIGHT

Boredom had officially set in which, for Robert, wasn't a bad thing. He needed the time to think, and that was impossible with everyone screaming at each other. He also knew the longer they were left alone, the better their chances of making it out alive. His hope was that whoever was doing this had their hands full dealing with several hundred people upstairs and would consider the nine of them a contained problem not worth focusing on right now.

The police had to be involved by now, which would mean the negotiation process had begun. Unfortunately, this also meant the clock was ticking. He knew they hadn't been locked in this room and left alone by accident. If demands were made and not met, the guys with guns would have to respond. And while dragging someone kicking and screaming out of a theater filled with 200 plus people created a whole host of operational and tactical issues, they had no such problems down here.

He surveyed the room thoroughly and, while there were quite a few things that might be useful as weapons in a hand-to-hand situation, these bad guys had guns. Of course if it came to that, something would be better than nothing but that wasn't a scenario he was willing to consider yet. This was no time to be a hero, he told himself. Heroes get themselves and the people around them killed.

Every so often, he quietly made his way over to the door and listened, trying to tell if there was a guard posted outside. He was fairly sure someone was there, not because heard anything but because, quite frankly, that's what he would have done.

The last time he was eavesdropping he noticed the door to the room was about twice the size of a normal doorway. It also opened out, which would have made a barricade useless. Tactically speaking, this situation sucked.

"You alright Mr. C.?"

"What?" he responded awkwardly, not realizing how deep in thought he was. "Oh, yes Dex. I'm fine."

"Good." Dex smiled. "Keep it together old man. Can't have you falling apart on me too." he slapped Robert on the shoulder, calmly walked past him...and started banging his fists on the door as hard as he could.

"Hey!" he shouted at the top of his lungs "Can a brother get a cheesesteak or somethin?!"

"Dexter!" Toshia yelled as Robert pulled him away from the door. "You need to stop playin!"

"But I'm hungry!" he whined dramatically, trying to get her to smile.

"I don't care." she grabbed him by the arm and lead him back to the sofa. "Those men have real guns."

"Ok, Ok! I get it." he conceded with a grin. "They real dudes wit real guns and all that. I get that. But come on Tosh, they could at least come up off a bag of sour cream. Right is right aint it?"

"Boy go sit your butt down somewhere." she replied, giving him the smile he worked so hard for.

"You guys close?" Lisa asked softly.

"She alright." Dex answered playfully.

"You can't tell?" Toshia smiled and sat down next to Lisa. "He's my best friend."

"That's awesome."

"Yeah it is." Toshia replied thoughtfully. "Our father was never around and mom died when he was nine. Since then, it's pretty much been the two of us."

"So you're raising him?"

"Since mom passed, yeah. Well, to be honest I'd say we're sort of raising each other. I had just turned 18 so it's not like I had all my stuff together you know?"

"How old are you now?"

"23."

"Wow." Lisa replied. "That is such an amazing story."

"I don't know about all that." Toshia shrugged. "You do what you have to you know? I could never let anything happen to him."

Lisa couldn't help but feel small. Here she was battling some sort of silly depression and the biggest problem in her life was, literally, the size of her butt. Talking with Toshia reminded her there were real people with real problems in the world.

"How y'all holding up?" asked Walter, as he sat down next to Lisa.

"We're good." Lisa smiled then rested her head on his shoulder.

"Well, you'll be doing even better in a second. Look what I found."

"Walter." Lisa laughed. "Where in the world did you find this?"

"I guess they stored the stuff for the concession stand down here. I found this box over by the door."

"Well don't let my brother see it." Toshia laughed.

"See what?" Dex asked, as he came over to where they were sitting. "Alright big man!" he shouted when he saw the box. "You my DUDE!"

He reached for the box but was unable to grab anything before Walter moved it out of his reach. "Come on big man stop playin!" he whined. "Hook a brother up!"

"I am Dex." Walter replied with a wink. "Don't you think you need to hook your girl up first?" he said, nodding in Lena's direction.

"Ok big man!" Dex whispered. "I like how you think."

Lena was sitting on the opposite side of the room with her mother, who was kneeling behind her and brushing her hair. Dex took the box over to where they were sitting, walked past Lena and offered it to Eleodora first.

"Kid has potential." Walter smiled.

"How would you know?" Lisa laughed playfully

"Takes a player to know a player." he smiled, then grabbed a couple bags of chips and tossed them over to Lisa, who immediately grabbed both bags and handed them to Toshia.

"You're not hungry?"

"I'm on a diet." Lisa smiled, almost embarrassed to admit it.

"Girl what are you trying to do? Disappear?" Toshia laughed, opening a bag for herself.

"I'm serious. We're going to Costa Rica and I want to look good."

"Costa Rica?" Toshia replied, impressed.

"Yep, for our three year anniversary."

"Wow. that's a long time."

"Yeah it is." Lena chimed in, coming over to join them. Her mother was happily chatting with Walter and Dex right now so she figured she'd stretch her legs.

"It doesn't really seem like a long time." Lisa replied softly. For her these last five years seemed more like weeks. Not that everything was perfect, because it definitely wasn't. It's just that, from about their third date, she had honestly forgotten what her life was like without him in it. They seemed to click together in all the ways that mattered and thinking about that brought a smile to her face.

"How did you meet?" Lena asked.

"We work at the same school. I'm a teacher, he's a counselor."

"Did he ask you out first?" Asked Toshia.

"God yes." Lisa laughed. "I don't think I would have had the guts to approach him."

"How did he do it?" Lena wanted to know.

"Well," Lisa smiled, remembering the day as she told the story. "We parked next to each other and one day he waited by his car pretending to be on the phone."

"Wait," Lena interrupted. "How did you know he was faking?"

"His phone rang! Mr. Player forgot to put it on vibrate."

The three of them shared a laugh and continued talking. Lisa wasn't normally the type to open up to strangers but found herself becoming genuinely fond of these girls. Their conversation went on for another few minutes as she shared more about her relationship and the two of them talked about the stuff girls talk about when men aren't around. As it turned out, this was exactly what she needed. Sitting there, chatting with Lena and Toshia completely took her mind away from everything and allowed her to relax for the first time since this nightmare began.

After another few minutes, Lena excused herself to go check on her mom.

"Lemme give y'all some privacy." Toshia smiled as Walter made his way back over.

"You ok?" he asked, sitting down after Toshia got up to check on her brother.

"I am now."

She lied down on her side and rested her head in his lap. She looked over at Toshia and Dex, who'd apparently found some playing cards and was now trying to convince his sister to play with him.

"They're good kids." he said softly, knowing exactly what she was thinking.

"Well, Toshia's not exactly a kid." Lisa corrected him. "She's 23."

"Wow," he replied, looking at her more closely. "She looks young."

"Yeah, and did you know she's raising him by herself?"

"Really?"

"Yep, they're mom died a few years ago."

"No father?"

"Apparently not, so Toshia had to step up when she was only 18 herself. Kinda makes you think huh?"

"Think about what?"

"I dunno." she responded thoughtfully "We go through life complaining about this and that, but come on. When you think about it, we don't have any real problems."

"Speak for yourself." he responded quickly. His tone caught her off guard.

"What's that supposed to mean?"

"Lisa, do you have any idea how many black kids are growing up without a father in this city?"

"I think I do." she answered defensively. "But what does that have to do with you?"

"You don't think a black man abandoning his family has anything to do with me?"

"No I don't."

"Well you're wrong."

"Wait a minute," she said, sitting up to make her point. "Just because your skin is the same color doesn't mean every bad thing another black person does is a reflection of you."

He shook his head.

"What?"

"Let's just drop it."

"Why?"

"Because it's a pointless conversation." he replied harshly. "You can't understand."

"Here we go again." she rolled her eyes. "Let me ask you this; Why do you stay with me if I'm so clueless?"

"I never said you were clueless."

"What would you call it?"

"Lisa," he said, trying to remain calm. "it's not an indictment of you to simply admit you have never walked in my shoes."

"And you've never walked in mine, but that doesn't mean I can't relate to what you're going through. Maybe not a hundred percent but still..."

"That's where we differ." he interrupted. "I honestly don't think you can."

"You are such a narcissist." she said firmly, not hiding her own frustration. "You think, as a woman, I have no idea what it's like to be discriminated against?"

"I don't think its the same thing and frankly, and please don't take this the wrong way, but frankly it's a little insulting to assume that because you're a good person you have some idea what it's like to be me."

"So because I'm white I'll never understand?"

"I'm sorry but I don't think it's possible."

"That's ridiculous." she replied, not buying it for a second. "Discrimination is discrimination Walter, nobody owns a patent on suffering."

"Nice speech. Now tell that to them."

It took her a moment to realize he was referring to Mark and Amber.

"What do they have to do with anything?"

"You think those two are unique?"

"I think they're idiots."

"And the world is full of idiots just like them."

It wasn't so much what he said that made her sad as it was the fact he wasn't getting her point. Whatever problems they had in the past, communication had never been one of them. She shook her head slowly.

"Walter," she said softly. "This has nothing to do with them."

"This has everything to do with them and anybody who thinks like them."

"Babe, this is about us."

"Us?" he replied, genuinely not understanding where she was coming from. "What are you talking about?"

"I'm talking about how you keep finding walls to put up between us that prevent us from moving forward."

He couldn't have been more confused if she had spoken in Mandarin Chinese. It was almost as if they had been having two separate conversations.

"How the hell did this become about us?"

"It's always been about us Walter." she replied, now struggling to keep her emotions in check. "I could, and would, do just about anything for you, but I can't change who I am."

"I never asked you to change anything Lisa."

"No, you just go out of your way to remind me I'm white every chance you get."

He looked at her in disbelief, knowing fully well what she was saying but not quite understanding how this particular conversation went there.

"I think we need to change the subject."

"I think you need to stop making up excuses and figure out what it is you want."

"Excuses for what?!" he shot back angrily. "What the hell are you talking about?"

"You want to keep making this about them," she replied. "But you have just as much of a problem with us being together as they do."

He was beginning to feel ambushed and, under normal circumstances, would have let her know how much he didn't appreciate it. But he knew this wasn't the time or place, so he did his best not to lose his temper.

"This is crazy." he said as calmly as he could. "Can you at least tell me what brought this on right now?"

"Look," she answered, trying to remain calm as well. "I'm not asking you to do anything you don't want to. I just don't understand why two people that love each other…"

"We've been through this." he interrupted. "It's not that simple."

"It is for me." she replied, firmly standing her ground. "And I told you when we met that I didn't want to spend years of my life on something that wasn't going anywhere…"

"Not going anywhere? That's ridiculous."

"I'm talking about whether or not you'll ever stop seeing the color of my skin and see me as the woman who loves you."

"Come on Lisa." he said, rolling his eyes. "Now is not the time to be having this discussion."

"Why not?"

"Because, in case you forgot, 'forever' has a slightly different meaning at the moment."

On the surface, there was nothing particularly harsh about what he said. Of course, under normal circumstances he would have had no reason to use those particular words, which is why she reacted the way she did. It would probably be an exaggeration to say she'd forgotten where they were but it had definitely been eased comfortably into the back of her mind. Now it all came flooding back to the front. She felt her pulse quickening.

"Whatever Walter." she said quietly. "I'm not trying to force you to do anything."

"I never said you were." he replied quietly, failing to mask his frustration. "I just don't want to talk about this right now."

"Ok," she said weakly. "We'll talk about it another time."

He was so relieved to be out of the conversation he never even noticed her anxiety had returned. Only this time, it came along with an intense sadness that had nothing to do with where they were or how they got there. Had he been paying closer attention, he might also have noticed something else.

While she clearly still loved him with all of her heart, there was no denying, in her mind, their relationship had just ended...

Lisa sat there in stunned silence until she started to feel claustrophobic. She needed to get the hell away from this room and these people and, yes, she needed to get away from Walter. But there was nowhere to go and the stress of being locked up in this room felt like it was eating away at her brain.

She stood up and walked over to the furthest corner where she leaned back against the wall and tried to steady herself. What she wouldn't give for a hot bath right now. She closed her eyes and imagined stepping into a tub full of hot water. She could almost feel the beads of sweat sliding down her forehead as she sank deeper into the tub and allowed all of her problems to melt away. If only it were that simple.

She felt lost. It was as if her world was falling down around her and all she could do was stand by and watch. She couldn't even say she wanted to go home anymore because, for the first time in over five years, she didn't really know where that was. She thought about her family and how much she needed to be with them right now. That would have to wait until she got out of here...IF she got out of here, she reminded herself.

The thought sent a chill through her, and just like that, she was terrified again. She looked around at the others, who all seemed to be doing fine, and wanted desperately to be as strong as they were. She wasn't even close.

The tears began as a trickle but quickly built into convulsive sobs. She breathed deeply and tried to will herself to be strong. It was pointless. She wasn't strong. She was weak and she hated herself for it.

She wanted it to be like in the movies where the heroine stands strong until the end. But she knew it wasn't going to happen like that. Not for her anyway. Her life was in the hands of the men outside that door and she knew she would beg them, she would plead to them on her knees, she would cry like a baby, she would say anything, she would DO anything to live.

The convulsions came suddenly. She threw herself onto her knees and retched into a nearby waste basket before anybody knew what was happening. Walter quickly rushed to her side to make sure she was ok. He held her hair and rubbed her back as wave after wave of nausea passed through her body, masking her hysterical sobbing. Lena found some towels somewhere and handed them to him as the nausea subsided.

Once he felt she was ok, he picked her up and carried her over the sofa where Dex and Toshia were now standing. They voluntarily moved to the side, allowing her a place to lie down. Walter knelt beside the sofa and held her hand as she cried. He wanted to make her feel better but realized there was nothing he could do. So he knelt there, holding her hand and caressing her face as she cried herself to sleep...

CHAPTER NINE

She was awake a few minutes before she opened her eyes. There was something peaceful about the darkness and, to be honest, she was embarrassed about breaking down like she did.

"You ok?" Lena asked as she sat up slowly on the sofa, still feeling a little light headed.

"I'm fine, I think." she smiled weakly. "Sorry about losing it before."

"Girl, please." Toshia smiled. "Tired as I am, I'm just mad I didn't think of it first."

She looked around and saw nothing much had changed while she was asleep. Walter was playing cards with Dex while Robert and Eleodora seemed to be chatting peacefully together by the door and Lena and Toshia were seated on the floor next to the sofa where she'd been sleeping. It was the kind of surreal picture she could see ending up as an artist portrayal of what it must have been like for the hostages as they awaited rescue.

She purposely avoided looking at Mark or Amber. She didn't need that headache right now. She was actually feeling better except for the horrible taste in her mouth.

"Walter, do you have any gum?"

"Here you go." he handed her a pack he had in his pocket. "You feeling ok?"

"Yea, I'll be fine." she said, shifting over on the sofa so he could join her. "I'm sorry."

"You have nothing to apologize for." he interrupted. "None of this is easy."

He put his arms around her and pulled her into his chest, knowing he couldn't make everything go away but at least wanting her to know he would take care of her, as he always did. There was no doubt in his mind how much he loved her. She was everything to him and had been that for a long time. The problem was everyone else and how they reacted to them being together. As much as he wanted to ignore all the chatter, he knew building a life with Lisa would be difficult for both of them, but mostly for her.

That's what she didn't see. He was perfectly equipped to deal with idiots like Mark and Amber, because he'd been dealing with them his whole life. As sad as it sounded, for him, that part came naturally.

For Lisa, none of this existed until she began dating him. Sure, she knew it was out there and had probably even seen or heard a lot of things that disgusted her. But it was never about her. Even now, despite the fact they were a couple, she was really only forced to deal with it when they were out somewhere together.

That would all change the minute they got married or had children and that is what scared him the most. She would no longer be able to live happily in her bubble where people were basically good. She would be kicked out of that exclusive club and, as much as she would say it didn't matter, he would always know different. It was one thing to hear someone called a name and to feel bad for them or feel disgusted by how some people treated others. It was another thing entirely to be called that name yourself or to have to explain to your children why they were being treated that way. Right now, she could put on a fake smile and deal with the funny looks and snide remarks whenever they went out to dinner or to a movie. But could she deal with that every time she left the house? Could she deal with not being able to escape it?

It was never a question of loving her, that much he was sure of. He just wasn't sure she knew what she was getting into and he could never live with himself if he didn't do everything he could to protect her. Even if that meant losing her.

"So Lena," Lisa asked, trying to lighten the mood. "I noticed your accent, where are you from?"

"Cuba."

"Were you born there?"

"Yes, we came to the states when I was 5."

"Just you and your mom?"

"Yes."

"That must've been hard for her."

"She left her entire family and all of her friends to come here and give me a better life." Lena acknowledged. "I owe everything to her."

"She was doing her job." Toshia said. "She's supposed to take care of you."

Lisa immediately realized that last statement was as much about Toshia and Dex as it was Lena and her mother. She was surprised how much she found herself liking Toshia and could see herself maintaining a friendship with her long after this was all over.

"And you Toshia? Where are you and Dex from?"

"Born and raised in West Philly."

"Oh really? We were thinking about moving into the city."

"So you guys live together?" Lena asked innocently.

"We do." Lisa smiled

"And he's taking you to Costa Rica for your anniversary?" Toshia asked.

"Yes and?"

"Nothing, I'm just saying." Toshia laughed. "Sounds like a great way to *ring* in your anniversary."

The girls shared a laugh while Walter shook his head. He wasn't about to get pulled back into this conversation, so he went over and refocused himself on his card game.

"Don't even pay no attention to them big man." Dex encouraged as he dealt a new hand. "The way I see it, your girl is fine. And if she breakin you off on a consistent basis you might as well do the right thing. Aint nothin out in them streets but trouble."

"Dexter." Toshia laughed loudly. "Boy you are 14 years old. What do you know about what's in 'them streets.' "

"Don't hate me cause I'm sexy Toshia."

"Yeah ok, sexy."

"Nobody said anything about getting married ok." Walter offered abruptly, trying to regain control of the conversation.

"God forbid." Lisa said softly.

"You messin up big man!" Dex exclaimed. "I'm telling you. Don't let the peanut gallery punk you."

"Dex," Lisa offered. "Walter has a little problem with the idea of forever."

"Is that what you think?" he asked.

"Dawg, your girl is FINE." Dex pleaded.

"Thank you dex." Lisa smiled. She could tell Walter had gotten a little attached to Dex and so it was fun seeing him put on the spot.

"So what's the problem big man?" Dex pressed.

"When the time is right." he replied lamely.

"Ok," Dex responded, unconvinced. "Study long study wrong."

"Can we change the subject please?"

It was more of a command than a question. Things were awkward enough between him and Lisa and this conversation couldn't be helping.

"Where is your new place?" Robert asked, trying to help him out.

"We were looking for something in Center City." Walter replied, relieved to be discussing anything besides his relationship. "Maybe close to the museum."

"You should look at Northern Liberties."

"We did at first, but the prices were kinda high for a couple of teachers. You live in the city?"

"Not anymore." he smiled. "The city life is for young people and I haven't been one of those in a while."

"You're only as old as you feel right?" Walter offered with a smile.

"And I feel anything but young." Robert laughed.

"Well you sure don't look like an old man." Lisa smiled. There was just something about Robert she liked. "So are you originally from the area?"

"No, I moved here in 75, when I got out of the military."

"Oh? Where are you from originally?"

"Boston right?" Mark responded out of nowhere.

Everyone in the room was stunned into silence. Amber, who was beginning to doze off, thought maybe she was dreaming; but when she noticed how the others were all staring at them, she knew they had heard the same thing she just did. The good news was that her mind had, at least for the moment, shifted away from the pain in her side. The bad news was she had no idea how, exactly, her husband knew this man.

As for Robert, his eyes were focused solely on Mark's. He wasn't quite as caught off guard as everyone else but had been hoping he wouldn't have to deal with this until after this was all over.

"You really don't have a clue do you?" Mark asked, his voice dripping with disgust.

"Mark?" Robert muttered almost imperceptibly. There were no words to describe exactly how he was feeling. Since the moment this all began, he had prepared himself to deal with whatever came next...but he wasn't ready for this. Not by a long shot.

"You really are a worthless piece of shit you know that?" Mark responded, his anger flooding to the surface. He had been holding it in all night but hearing this asshole go on about the great life he was leading was too much for him to take.

"Mark," Amber prodded gently. "what's going on?"

She looked at her husband expectantly but he said nothing. She had never seen him like this. He was completely fixated on this guy and she had no idea why.

"Mr. C." Dex asked. "You know this dude?"

They stood there for what seemed like an hour before Robert responded. Truth be told, he didn't know what to say.

"Mark is my son."

"Get the fuck outta here!"

"DEXTER!" Toshia, Lisa and Eleodora shouted.

"My bad." he apologized and sat back down next to his sister who gave him a slap in the head.

"Everyone meet Mark Cohen. My only child."

The words seemed to come out involuntarily. He tried desperately to think of something else to say but came up with nothing. He, like everyone else, just stood there in awkward, stunned silence.

"Mark, is this true?" Amber broke the silence. She was embarrassed he would hide something like this from her and now she wanted answers. "You need to tell me what's going on." she pleaded.

He said nothing.

"Hold up Mr. C." Dex approached slowly. "Not for nothin but, you know, I thought you was, you know...I thought you was like...gay."

"That's none of your business Dexter." Robert replied weakly, as he sat down suddenly feeling old and very tired.

"Nah, it's cool," Dex smiled "I'm just sayin."

"Yep." Mark said abruptly. "My dad the fag. And he's proud of it no less."

"Yo! How you gonna call your pops a fag?!"

"It's ok Dex." Robert said softly.

"It's the truth." Mark replied sharply

"So you hate your own father too?" Toshia asked. She assumed it would be impossible to hate this clown any more than she already did. Apparently she was wrong.

"You can't choose your parents." Amber offered unconvincingly, still trying to make sense of the situation.

"You have any idea what it's like growing up with a fag for a father?!"

"Now is not the time Mark." Robert said quietly.

"Bullshit now aint the time! Its been the right freakin time for 20 years!"

"I can't change the past."

Robert wanted this to go away, at least for now. But he knew that was wishful thinking. His son had gone through a lot of trouble to 'run into him' tonight so he was probably determined to deal with this on his terms, not Roberts.

"You think I want you to change the past?" Mark asked hatefully. "Why? So you can have a second chance? So you can come home and read me stories or play catch? Please! I don't need you. I've NEVER needed you!! The only reason I came here tonight was to tell you I buried my mother yesterday and that I hoped you died a lonely pitiful old man!"

The words stung, of course, but Robert knew he had earned every single one of them. He wanted to respond but honestly didn't know where to begin and couldn't afford to spend too much time figuring it out. Now was not the right time to be dealing with any of this. Unlike everyone else, his mind never strayed too far from where they were and his focus was still on getting through this night alive.

"Mark." he said calmly, trying to be as non-confrontational as possible. "I know you're pissed off but we can't do this here."

"Why not Mr. C?" he replied sarcastically. "You said we don't need to panic right?"

"Look, there is nothing I can say that…"

"You're goddamn right there's nothing you can say!"

"You don't think I know that?" Robert replied, struggling to maintain his composure. "Look, I am not perfect and have never claimed to be…"

"But it's ok for you to judge me though right?" Mark interrupted. "Mr. C is such a great guy right? How can he have such an evil son right? Give me break! ...Why don't you tell em the truth pop?!"

"Because they don't care!" Robert shouted in frustration. "Look around! You think anybody in this room gives a damn about you or your problems right now?! None of this has anything to do with anybody in this room

besides you and me! And in case you haven't noticed, this isn't our living room! We are being held in this room against our will and the only thing you need to be concerned with is getting out of here alive so PLEASE. I'm asking you to table this and lets deal with it later."

"Sorry gay boy but you don't get to tell me what to do."

"Alright look." Robert replied sternly. "I've asked you twice. Now I'm telling you...let this go."

"And if I don't? What are you gonna do gay boy?"

"You've called me that twice now." Robert said firmly. "There won't be a third time."

"You think I'm scared of you?"

"Mark, I am telling you for the last time..."

"What? You gonna beat me up?" he replied with a sarcastic laugh. "Get in line. If you'd been around you'd know I got my ass kicked practically every day when I was a kid. Oh but you weren't around were you? That's right! You were too busy looking for someone to stick a..."

The move came so quickly it caught everyone off guard. In what seemed like a split second, Robert was out of his seat and had thrown a perfectly placed forearm into Mark's right shoulder, spinning him to the ground in a heap so fast his wife didn't have a chance to scream. He knew his reflexes seemed impressive to the untrained eye but the truth was, he had measured the distance between him and his son early on in the conversation when it became clear he wouldn't be able to settle him down with words alone. Whatever empathy he felt for the son he abandoned would have to be set aside until they were out of this room. And, as much as he hated doing it, if the only way to get him to focus was to knock him on his ass, well, that's just what had to be done.

Before anyone could react he lifted Mark off the ground by the back of his shirt and spun him around so he could look him directly in the eye.

"Now you WILL shut up or I will shut you up." he said firmly, but without a hint of anger or agitation. He was clearly in his comfort zone once things turned physical.

"Let him go." Amber demanded. She wasn't about to sit there and let anyone manhandle her husband, even if he was a lying bastard.

Having made his point, Robert let go of his shirt and walked away. Mark immediately clutched his right shoulder and fell to the ground, where he didn't even attempt to get up.

The room fell silent yet again. Robert tried clearing his head but couldn't shake free of the magnitude of what was happening. Try as he might, he couldn't stop himself from thinking back to all the things he wished he had done differently. Living a life without regret was a nice cliche that probably worked for some, but had no bearing whatsoever on his personal reality. He had lived with nothing but for most of his adult life.

He remembered the awesome responsibility he felt when he brought his wife and newborn son home from the hospital. He remembered how excited, and scared, he was. And now, after almost 20 years, he was standing face-to-face with living, breathing proof of how much he had failed.

He kept his eyes fixed on the floor in front of him so as to avoid making eye contact with anyone. He felt like all of their eyes were on him, waiting for an explanation. An explanation he didn't have.

"I never said I was perfect." he said, to no one in particular. "I've made mistakes like everybody else...But I've tried to learn to take responsibility for the things I've done. I made my choices and I have to live with them..."

"You don't have to explain yourself." Toshia said softly.

"I don't want anyone thinking I'm something I'm not." he continued. "I spent most of my life hiding, afraid of what people would say or think. Unfortunately for part of that time, I wasn't living for myself. I had a wife and child. I told myself I had to live that lie for them but in the end, the only one I was fooling was myself...they ended up getting hurt in the process."

His voice trailed off at the end. He knew the words would ring hollow the second they came out of his mouth. At the same time, he felt he had to try and say something. Unfortunately, there were no words that could measure up to the mistakes he had made in his past. He closed his eyes and sighed deeply.

"You do realize you're not fooling anybody right?"

"I'm not trying to Mark."

"So you accept responsibility for what you did to me?"

"You are a grown man." Toshia chimed in, having heard enough.

"Stay out of it!" Mark shouted angrily, then turned his attention back to Robert. "C'mon pop, say it. Are you sorry for lying to me my whole life? Are you sorry for abandoning me? Are you sorry for..."

"I never meant to hurt you." Robert interrupted.

"Screw your intentions! You think I can't see through your bullshit?! If you're looking for forgiveness, you better look somewhere else because you have NONE coming from here."

"You," Toshia said after a moment. "are a miserable ass."

"Why don't you mind your own business?"

"Why don't YOU stop blaming the world because you're miserable?"

"I didn't choose my father."

"And you father didn't CHOOSE to be gay!"

"So what if he didn't?! He damn sure used it as an excuse to abandon his wife and kid!"

"He's your FATHER!" Toshia screamed. "He was born gay in a society that is openly hostile towards gays; so much so he felt like he had to run away from who he was..."

"Oh bullshit!" Mark erupted, waving his hand in Toshia's direction. "So Mr. Big Bad marine has to run and hide in a corner because somebody might be mean to him? ...Please...you think I didn't wanna run? What about my mother? But we didn't get to run away did we? We had to stay behind and deal with the bullshit HE left behind."

There was no denying the bastard had a point. Toshia knew, first hand, what it was like growing up without a father but at least hers was never around. She and Dex never had to suffer through the indignity of watching him leave. She could only imagine the impact that kind of rejection would have on a young boy.

"Ok, so you suffered because your father wasn't around," Toshia conceded. "I get that, believe me. But now you've grown up to become part of the reason he thought he had to leave in the first place! What kind of sense does that make?"

"About as much sense as blaming someone for who their parents are."

Amber was in no mood to defend her so-called husband but there was only so much of this liberal garbage she could listen to. It always amazed her how far liberals would go to excuse the bad behavior of anyone on the left.

"This country," she continued. "is being led straight to hell by queers, and race traitors, with their inter-species relationships and queer marriages...You all say we preach hate?! But what about compassion for the kids these freaks have. What do you think their lives are like?"

"So you're worried about the kids?" Toshia asked incredulously.

"Somebody has to be." Amber responded.

"Well, here's something to think about. If it wasn't for people like YOU, there would probably be nothing to worry about!"

Toshia was done. She'd been locked in this room for god knows how long and desperately needed to get away from these people. The ugliness of the conversation combined with the reality of the situation had begun to take its toll. She managed to hold it together until now mostly because she knew she had to, ...but now the walls were slowly beginning to close in on her and she had no idea how to make them stop..

She closed her eyes and tried to calm herself, realizing now was not the time to be having an anxiety attack. Still, she knew if she didn't get a break from all the tension she was going to snap. She took a deep breath and tried to force her mind to go elsewhere...

"Dammit!" Mark shouted abruptly, feeling like a caged animal himself. "I need to get the FUCK outta here!"

"We all do." said Lena softly, voicing what they were all feeling.

"Nobody's talkin to you."

"Don't be talkin to my girl like that." Dex said, smiling at Lena the entire time.

"I'm not your girl Dex." she replied shyly

"Don't be frontin cause your moms is here…" he replied with a smile. "you know you feelin a brother…"

"Not as much as you feelin yourself…" Toshia added dryly, getting a much needed laugh from the others.

"I see you got jokes today."

"I'm just playin with you little brother." she replied apologetically, giving him a hug.

The light hearted exchange seemed to be exactly what the room needed. Lisa was especially thankful for the shift in energy.

"So Lena," she said, anxious to keep the positive vibe going. "Do you have a boyfriend?"

"Lena is here to get an education." Eleodora answered sternly.

"She couldn't get an education in her own country?" Mark asked sarcastically.

"That's enough." Robert said firmly, not wanting the conversation to go down that road again.

"You gonna stop me?" Mark replied defiantly.

"No these fools ain't about to get to brawlin up in this piece." Dex laughed, earning a hard slap in the back of the head from Toshia.

"Stop!" he whined. "You play too much."

"Well stop instigating."

Mark glared at them and shook his head. As much as he hated the man, he realized his so-called father was right. This was no time to be playing out some family drama. Still, he could feel the anger building up inside and knew he needed to calm himself down. A quick glance around the room at the assortment of degenerates he was stuck with made him realize that would be easier said than done.

"Is that why you lied?" Amber asked, as quietly as possible, so that only Mark would hear.

"What are you talking about?"

"You know exactly what the hell I'm talking about." she replied tersely, struggling not to raise her voice. "I asked you, twice, why it was so god-awful important to come to this thing tonight and both times, you looked me right in the eye and lied. I guess I shouldn't be surprised."

"What is that supposed to mean?"

"It means, you've done nothing but lie since the day I met you."

"That's not true." he replied calmly, not wanting to inflame the situation any further."I never told you about my father because I wanted nothing more to do with him."

"And because you didn't want me to know the truth about who you are, Mr. Cohen."

"That's his name, not mine."

"How convenient." she replied sarcastically.

"Amber stop it. You know exactly who I am."

"I do now." she replied coldly, looking him square in the eye. She wanted there to be no question in his mind as to what she was trying to say. There wasn't.

He'd seen the look before and it always gave him the chills. His wife had an uncanny ability to communicate silently and her most recent message was coming through to him loud and clear. Before he could say anything, she looked away in disgust, leaving him feeling more isolated and alone than he would have thought possible.

The flood of emotion hit him like a wave and, literally, almost knocked him off his feet. Amber was the only family he had left and even the thought of losing her made him feel like he was dying. He was a heartbeat away from breaking down in tears but he refused to give any of his roommates the satisfaction.

He looked around the room, trying to compose himself, and made brief eye contact with Robert who was sitting by himself with his back up against the front door. In an instant, every emotion he was feeling turned into anger. It was as if someone flipped a switch in his brain and activated his full capacity for hatred directed at one individual.

"I hope you die." he spit out venomously, never taking his eyes off of his father.

"What is the matter with you?!" Eleodora shouted instantly, appalled by what she was hearing.

"Mind your business old lady."

"Mark, cut it out." Robert said firmly

"Don't tell me what to do faggot."

The room fell silent and everyone's eyes shifted over to Robert. Walter was especially curious how he would react as he'd already knocked his son on his ass once for calling him a name. He warned him not to call him that word and, judging the way he carried himself, Walter didn't think Robert was a guy who made idle threats.

"You are disgusting." said Eleodora.

"Who cares what you think?" Mark replied quickly. "Besides, my country, my rules. You don't like it, go back to Castro."

"You do realize this is a nation of immigrants?" Walter asked condescendingly.

"Yeah and that's exactly the problem you idiot." Mark replied.

"No." said Robert loudly, clearly tiring of hearing Mark's mouth. "The problem is the more you speak the more ignorant you sound." .

"Nobody asked you fag boy."

Out of nowhere, even before Robert had a chance to respond, Toshia picked up a half eaten bag of pretzels and threw the contents in Marks face. She stood up, glaring at him as if she was daring either him or his wife to do anything about it.

Mark looked over at Amber, who didn't move. The way she was feeling right now she was just mad she didn't think of throwing something at the lying sonofabitch first.

Mark looked back at Toshia and gave her a dirty look. He couldn't believe this ape had the audacity to throw food at him. Just goes to show why they keep them in glass cages at the zoo, he thought. Sill, this little tramp needed to be set straight.

"Don't do that again." he said menacingly.

Ha!" Toshia laughed loudly. "And what are YOU gonna do if I do?"

"Try me and you'll..."

Before he could finish his sentence, there was another bag of food flying in is face, though this time Toshia couldn't find any more pretzels, so she used chips instead.

"I'm waiting." she said, smiling at him defiantly.

He had been embarrassed one too many times today and wasn't about to let this one go. He stood up out of his seat and...

"Boy, you take one more step and I will work you like a Mexican at a car wash."

Walter was the first one to laugh, followed quickly by the rest of the room. He had noticed the look on Mark's face and had already positioned himself between the midget and Toshia, on the off chance he decided to go mental. He also assumed Dex would step up to defend his sister and wanted to be in position to control that situation as well. What he didn't see coming was Dex's comment, which caught him so off guard he really couldn't do anything but laugh.

Lisa and the others quickly followed suit and, in an instant, the room was filled with laughter and the mood appeared to have changed yet again. Unfortunately the laugh they were sharing was, for the most part, joyless. The constant emotional back and forth was seriously testing the limits of their sanity so, while Dex's comment was funny, their reaction to it was awkwardly exaggerated. It was almost as if they saw the opportunity to laugh together as some kind of reprieve. Each of them was, in their own way, so desperate for a break that any light-hearted moment would have been blown up to be some kind of oasis in the middle of a barren desert. And they ran to it as fast as they could.

Dex, for his part, smiled proudly when he saw everyone laughing; even though he could tell it was slightly forced. He had been trying to lighten the mood but they had all been way too uptight...until now.

He quickly jumped to his feet, bolted over to the corner and started loudly digging through one of the boxes, tossing things out onto the floor recklessly. He was making a terrible racket and Robert was about to say something but, looking around the room, thought better of it. No one else had any better idea than he did what Dex was looking for and they didn't seem to care. In fact, he noticed they seemed to be more curious than anything else.

By this point, they were so far removed from how this all started that he figured his biggest concern was no longer the guys with the guns. His major issue at this moment was the hidden toll stress was taking on their states of mind. He could see the desperate look in their eyes, even if they couldn't recognize it themselves. Fear, boredom and the mind-numbing monotony of being cooped up in this room for hours upon hours with no end in sight was beating them down mentally.

His son and daughter in-law had provided a useful distraction at first, but the constant drama was draining. Whatever Dex had in mind, and the kid obviously had a plan, it would probably be a welcome diversion.

"There it is baby!" Dex exclaimed happily, as he found what he was looking for.

"Music?!" Mark practically screamed in disbelief as Dex held up an old portable CD player he found buried in one of the prop boxes.

"Aw stop bein a punk." Dex replied, looking for an outlet to plug it in. "They probably aint thinking about us."

"You're not serious?!" Mark looked around the room at the others, amazed no one was saying anything. He made eye contact with Robert and could tell he was uneasy as well.

"Come on," he pleaded, his voice shaky with fear. "this kid's gonna get us killed!"

"Dex, what are you doing?" Toshia asked cautiously.

"I'm not doing anything." he responded mischievously. "WE are gonna teach these poor, lost souls some line dances."

"Do you have to do this?" Amber asked, clearly uncomfortable with what was about to happen.

"Look," Dex replied confidently. "Aint no sense in just sitting here waiting for the boogie man to show up. You gotta live every day like it's your last right?"

"Do this and it might just be." Amber said softly, shaking her head in disbelief.

"Well," he replied, picking up another bag of chips. "I can't think of a better way to go out than with a bag of sour cream and a funky ass jam."

He looked around the room and could see everyone was still a bit uneasy. "Y'all do what you want." he said, not wanting to lose his crowd. "I'm gonna get my groove on."

And with that he started looking around for an outlet. He was looking over against the far wall, behind some wood planks but couldn't find anything.

"Try behind the sofa." Walter said as he stood up and looked himself. Lisa looked over at him cautiously and he smiled. He figured there was no harm in having a little fun. His smile made her feel better and, after a few moments Robert, Toshia and Lisa were up, looking for an outlet before Dex found one on the wall behind Amber's chair.

Rather than ask her to move, which he knew she wouldn't, he crawled on the floor, squeezed his arm behind the recliner and plugged in the extension cord. He hopped to his feet, grabbed the cd player, plugged it in and then started to clear out some space in the middle of the room to use as a dance floor. Lena, after getting a nod of approval from Eleodora, quickly joined the others and started helping.

Amber couldn't believe what she was seeing. She would have put up more of a fight but realized there was no point. They would be incapable of understanding anything that wasn't dumbed down to their level and she was in no mood to try and convince some undisciplined primates not to get themselves killed. Better them than her, she thought.

She gingerly stood up from her chair, wanting to get as far away from these idiots as she could. Mark saw that she was struggling and offered his hand to help. She ignored him and moved away from the chair, toward the door. She was obviously still in great pain so he instinctively took her arm to assist and was slapped hard across the face.

"Don't touch me." she said coldly, giving him an icy stare that left no doubt how serious she was. When she felt she had made her point, she turned her back to him and made her way to a folding chair close to the front door. She sat down, looked up and saw him staring at her. She imagined he was trying to come up with some other lie he could tell her to get out of this. They made eye contact and she held her stare long enough for him to realize there was nothing there. It was almost as if she was looking through him, showing no emotion at all.

What he couldn't see; what she would never allow him to see; was how devastated she was. She felt as if her heart was physically breaking as she stared at him from across that room and, while she wanted to hate him forever for what he did to her, she knew it would never be that simple.

The truth is, she was pregnant. She had been waiting for the right time to tell him, having only found out herself a week before his mom died, but the opportunity hadn't yet presented itself. And now, what should have been the happiest time in their lives, had been turned into the worst nightmare imaginable, all because of him.

She was furious and wanted to tell him exactly how she felt but she was afraid if she went down that road right now he would see the truth. And that was that, as much as she might deny it, she still loved him. For almost five years now, he was the first person she thought of when she woke up in the morning and the last person she thought of before she fell asleep at night. Their wedding, five years ago, was the happiest day of her life and not just because she got to dress up like a princess. She cried tears of joy on that afternoon because her heart was filled with a love she didn't even know existed. She was one of the lucky ones who found her soul mate and she made a promise before god to love and honor and cherish him forever.

His name was Cohen, she thought to herself.

She had never felt so conflicted about anything in her life and it was making her nauseous. She rested her head in the palms of her hands and tried to relax. After a moment, she made herself look down at the ground and cover her eyes. She didn't want to risk him seeing her tears.

"**Alright**, y'all ready?" Dex asked.

"Get your teach on young man." Walter responded playfully, as they all stood in a line behind Dex.

Mark tried his best to ignore them. He wanted to reach out to his wife but didn't know what to say. He never meant for her to find out about any of this, especially not like this, but it was too late to worry about any of that now. He just had to find a way to fix it, which would be much easier said than done.

He knew she was pissed, but this was something different. They way she looked at him was no different than the way she looked at the rest of these animals. His heart started racing as he became desperate at the thought of losing her. He had to make her see this wasn't his fault and that he was still the same guy she fell in love with.

He didn't even realize he was shaking. His entire body felt like it was being violently tossed back and forth; as if he was standing flat foot on the deck of a ship in a hurricane.

He knew he had to calm himself, so he sat down in the recliner and closed his eyes. He breathed deeply and assessed the situation. Yes, he would have some explaining to do and no, it wouldn't be easy. But, more than anything else, he knew they loved each other. He would just need time to remind her of that. As soon as they got out of here, he would take her away on a long vacation where they could be alone and reconnect. Yea, this would all work out fine. He even had the perfect place in mind. A client had a cabin in Wyoming on a private ranch that was absolutely beautiful in the fall. He'd make the call as soon as...

CHAPTER TEN

Amber was the first to react but by the time she heard the footsteps over Dex's music, there was nothing she could do. The door had flung open violently and, before she could get out of the way, she was yanked to her feet by her hair.

"Get off me!!" she screamed hysterically as she was thrown hard up against the wall.

"Whoa whoa whoa!" Mark protested frantically before receiving a forearm to the chest that sent him reeling to the ground.

The entrance happened so abruptly none of the others had a chance to panic, which probably saved their lives Robert thought to himself. The hostages moved, in unison, toward the far corner of the room as two gunmen moved aggressively in their direction, weapons firmly at their shoulders. It seemed like they were driving them into the very corner they were instinctively retreating into anyway.

The decisive nature of their movements told Robert this crew was much better trained than the first group. He cursed himself for abandoning his post by the door but there was nothing he could do about that now.

"What did I fucking tell you?!" Mark screamed at Dex, near tears. He was still on the floor staring up at the mountain of a man who'd just knocked him down before turning his attention to the two men manhandling his wife behind him.

"Leave her alone man…c'mon!!" he pleaded desperately as got to his knees.

Ignoring him, one of the assailants put a hand on Amber's throat and slowly started to squeeze. Not hard enough to cut off her air, but firmly enough to let her know who was in control.

"Let go of me." she said, squirming weakly and receiving a hard slap in the face for resisting. The flood of adrenaline coursing through her veins served to mute the pain somewhat, but she knew that wouldn't last very long. Eventually it would wear off and her entire body would hurt like hell…assuming she lived long enough.

"We told him not to play the music!" Mark pleaded, hysterically pointing at Dex. "He…he wouldn't listen!! It aint our fault!!! Take him!!!!"

He was completely beside himself. His hands were shaking violently and he felt light headed but, even as panic overwhelmed him, he knew he had to do something. He tried to get to his feet and was immediately met with a boot to the chest, knocking him back to the ground where he laid motionless.

"Mark stay down!" Robert commanded, his muscles tensing. Seeing some guy twice his size knock his kid to the floor made him want to react. Unfortunately he had already assessed the situation and concluded he had no options.

The two men in front of them had been sure to keep the proper distance, making it impossible to get to either one of them in a single movement. A simple flinch in either direction would have earned him little more than a bullet in the chest so he told himself to lay back. The problem was he didn't think he had it in him to stand there and watch these animals shoot his son.

"Please don't hurt him!" Amber screamed, tears flowing freely down her face, forgetting for a moment everything she just learned. She didn't care about his lies or his past or who or what he was supposed to be. None of that mattered right now. The only thing that mattered in that moment was the man she loved; her best friend. The man she woke up to every morning. The man she laughed with and cried with. The man she wanted to have a family with...in that moment she realized how much she really loved him. She knew now what mattered and, more importantly, what didn't. It broke her heart that she would never get to tell him…

"Let her go you fucking pig!" Mark shouted weakly, as he struggled to sit up.

"What did you say?"

They had agreed earlier not to speak in front of the hostages but Omer couldn't resist. This was the bitch that shot Xavier and he had been looking forward to this moment ever since. He nodded to his partner, who tightened his grip on Amber's throat enough to make her squirm but not enough to cut off her circulation…not yet.

He approached Mark slowly, never taking his eyes off him. When he was close enough, he leaned over and whispered in his ear. "Do you have something to say?"

"Let her go please!" Mark begged, crying hysterically and cursing himself for being so weak. "I'll do whatever you want. Please don't hurt her."

Amber closed her eyes, unable to watch him beg these animals for her life. She just wanted one more minute to tell him she forgave him and that she would always love him. To see him in so much pain and not be able to do anything about it was almost too much for her to take. She summoned what little strength she had left and struggled mildly against her assailants hand until she was cowed by the feel of cold steel pressed hard up against her forehead. She opened her eyes wide, saw the gun and found herself face to face with a terrorist. He was wearing a black ski mask to hide his identity so only his eyes were visible...that was enough.

She had never seen such pure malevolence before. The man held her gaze until she looked down, not wanting to look too much further into the soul of the devil. He leaned forward and whispered in here ear

"It was always going to be you we took first..."

The words sent a chill up her spine and she felt her body go limp as she began to accept her fate. Then, in an odd moment of clarity, she realized something was off about his voice. In fact, it wasn't just this guy. She noticed the same thing when the other one spoke. It was almost as if something was missing. Oh my god! she thought to herself as her eyes opened wide in amazement....

"Do you suggest I take you instead?" Omer asked menacingly. He had no intention of letting this bitch go but he wanted to see how far her husband would go to save her. As he expected, Mark said nothing

"Your time will come." he said quietly then stood up and, unceremoniously, walked away. He and his partner grabbed Amber by her arms and dragged her toward the door.

"NOOO! PLEASE!!!!" she screamed, crying and clawing at the walls hysterically. She knew it was pointless but the fear of death consumed her and made her fight with everything she had.

Mark just sat there, crying uncontrollably, until they finally managed to get her out of the room.

The whole scene took less than a minute but was horribly difficult to watch. It was so bad that Lisa buried her head crying in Walter's chest while Eleodora covered Lena's eyes to prevent her from seeing what was going on. Each of them knew instantly they would be haunted forever by the sounds of Amber's screams. Of course, forever had a slightly different meaning at the moment...

The two gunmen holding them in the corner slowly backed away toward the door, never lowering their weapons for even a second. When they were close to the door, the guy holding Mark retreated with them, only he didn't back away slowly. He lowered his weapon, turned his back to Mark, and simply walked out the door.

CHAPTER ELEVEN

Acute stress reaction, or ASR, is a psychological condition arising in response to a traumatic event and should not be confused with 'shock,' the unrelated medical condition having to do with circulation. Technically, ASR is a variation of Post-Traumatic Stress Disorder, most commonly associated with combat veterans. It is triggered by exposure to an extreme trauma that causes intense fear, usually involving threats to life or serious injury.

People suffering from acute stress often become detached from their surroundings. They act as if they are in a daze because they are intently focused on flashbacks or images in their head of the traumatic event. Other symptoms are varied but typically include agitation, anxiety, impaired judgement, disorientation, detachment, and depression…all of which applied to Mark Cohen at the moment.

He had been crying and shaking uncontrollably since the door closed. He tried to compose himself but every time he closed his eyes to relax, all he could see was the anguished look on his wife's face as they dragged her away. He could still see the small traces of blood on the wall where she was scratching and clawing, trying to keep them from taking her away. He could so vividly hear her screams that it felt as if she was still in the room, but none of that is what haunted him the most.

What was haunting him the most was the fact that he had done nothing to help her. The woman he loved more than anything; the only family he had left; his best friend and confidante had been dragged away by thugs with guns and the best he could do was get on his hands and knees to beg them to let her go. His weakness disgusted him as much as he was sure it amused his attackers. He would never be able to look at himself in the mirror again without asking himself what kind of man has his wife taken away and does nothing to stop it?

He pictured the animals that took her sitting in some Afghani cave somewhere, laughing at how pathetic he was. He imagined them joking with each other about what a coward he had been and telling their partners stories about how they knocked him down and left him crying on the floor like a baby. The more he dwelled on it the more infuriated he became. Thinking about all that had been taken from him and then picturing the people responsible still breathing, much less laughing or enjoying themselves, awakened a rage in him that had been slowly building since the scene in the lobby. He was fed up with feeling powerless. What was happening to him would never stop unless he did something about it. They would have to pay.

Right then and there, he realized he would never truly know peace again. The rest of his life would be haunted by the images of this night and, he resolved to himself, if it would be that way for him it had to be that way for them. No, he corrected himself. That's not good enough. Justice demanded that they not have it as bad as he would...they needed to have it much worse. In fact, he was going to make it his mission in life to see to it.

With each breath he could feel the change occurring within him. At first his desire for vengeance seemed normal, considering what he'd been through. But as his thirst for revenge grew, it began to ferment his anger, turning it into something else, something more familiar...hatred. For Mark Cohen, pure unadulterated hatred was a familiar and potent narcotic with the ability to mask all levels of physical or emotional pain. And, much like any other powerful opiate, it was extremely addictive.

But that didn't matter right now because he desperately needed what his go-to drug had to offer. He needed to somehow make sense of his situation and the more he allowed hatred to fill his heart and flow freely through his veins, the more comfortable he became. He could much better accept what was going on as long as he first accepted it was happening simply because they hated him. This made perfect sense, in his mind, because he now knew how much he hated them.

Slowly but surely clarity of thought returned to his brain and he began to see an alternate future for himself, one with a defined and righteous purpose...

"What up Fam?" Toshia asked, putting her arm around Dex and holding him tightly. She did this as much to ease her own trembling as to comfort her younger brother.

"Aint nothin fam." he replied softly. "How you livin?"

"Things is kinda rough right now, you know?"

She knew he was having trouble dealing with what they had all just witnessed. She was too. But her fear would have to be set aside for right now. Dex was her little brother and the only thing that mattered was making sure he was ok.

"This is a trip." he said, shaking his head as if to get the images to go away.

"Aint it though. You remember what mommy used to say?"

"Every time you turn around." he said with a smile, slowly shaking his head like their mom used to do. "But we gon' be alright. You know why?"

"Cause we family." Toshia finished the thought. "And don't nothing come before family."

"You damn skippy!"

Dex rewarded his big sister with a genuine smile. That, she thought to herself, was the amazing thing about her brother. He had been through so much in his young life and yet he always seemed to come out with a smile on his face. Almost every adult in his life had found some way to let him down but he kept on going. He was smart and funny, though not nearly as funny as he thought he was, and had a huge heart. He deserved better than he had been given in his life and she was determined to make sure he received it...nobody was going to hurt her little brother. Period.

"You ever miss mommy?" she asked, after a long moment.

"Sometimes..." he sat up to look at her in the eye. "I know it was rough. I mean, takin care of me and all that..."

"Boy don't even go there." she said firmly. "You're my brother."

"Well, Thank you anyway."

"You my peoples right?"

"You damn skippy!" he laughed and gave his sister an enthusiastic hug. A little too enthusiastic as the force of his embrace sent the two of them tumbling over onto their sides where Toshia's back lightly brushed up against Mark's leg. He had been completely lost in his own world until Toshia's inadvertent bump abruptly snapped him out of his daze and reminded him where he was and who he was there with.

"Ugh." he grunted in disgust then stood up and walked to the far corner of the room. Beyond being annoyed at having his fantasies of revenge interrupted, the absolute last thing he needed to see right now was anyone being happy and together. After everything that had happened to him, all he wanted was to get as far away from the others as these four walls would allow.

"You ok?" Robert asked, joining him in the corner and, again, interrupting his internal dialogue.

Mark only partially heard the question and took a long pause before responding, almost as if he was feeling the words before allowing them to escape his lips.

"I swear to god," he began slowly, his eyes still burning and red from crying. "If anything happens to her I will kill every one of those fuckers myself."

"Don't jump to any conclusions." Robert cautioned. "There is every chance they just took her to another room to interrogate her or something." He knew, even as the words were coming out of his mouth, that they were complete bullshit. Still, he felt like he had to say something to reassure his son.

"Yeah right." Mark responded through yet more tears, not buying any of it for a second. "They probably just wanted her help with the drapes."

"We don't know anything for sure."

"Would you get your head out of your ass!" he exploded, startling the others. "Do you think these freaks are here to play games?!"

"Exactly my point." Robert pushed back. "If they wanted to kill us, they wouldn't waste time dragging us out of here one by one."

"Whatever, so we just sit here and see what happens next?"

"You have a better idea?" Robert asked, the concern in his voice was obvious.

Mark said nothing. Instead, he stood there and retreated back into his shell where he could fully indulge his anger. This was his 'happy place'. The place where he could live out his fantasies of the violence and carnage that would one day be reaped upon his enemies in the name of vengeance.

"Mark," Robert prodded gently. "What are you thinking?"

He was starting to become increasingly concerned about his son's state of mind. He felt horrible for what he had gone through but this night wasn't over yet; not by a long shot. And, if they were going to get through this, he needed to keep him from doing anything stupid.

"The next time that motherfucker comes through the door," Mark answered after a long pause. "You'll see what I'm thinking."

"That might be the dumbest thing you've said tonight." Walter responded harshly from across the room.

"Well, I aint gonna just sit here and wait to be taken away by some sand nigger."

Walter was no combat veteran or anything but he didn't have to be to look at Mark's fragile state and realize the guy was about to lose it. He also knew anything this idiot did could easily get the rest of them killed so it was in their best interest to snap him back into reality.

"You have some kind of death wish?"

"I'd rather die fighting like a man than sitting here like a freakin slave."

"You're unbelievable…" Toshia replied nervously. She saw what was going on as well and was also afraid of him lashing out and doing something crazy.

"What?" Robert asked, his frustration beginning to show. "Are you some kind of tough guy all of a sudden?"

The implication from Robert was not at all lost on Mark. Unfortunately the insult only served to steel his resolve even further. He was not a coward and would not leave this room being seen as one by either the terrorists or the low lives he was locked in this room with. Whatever he had to do they would ALL respect him before this was all over…

"You'll see. You'll ALL see."

"You don't know what happened to Amber!" Robert shouted, desperately trying to get through to him. "Would you at least think about that before you go and get yourself killed?!"

"What do you care if I get myself killed?!" Mark screamed, almost hysterically, in response. "If you had stopped the homeboys from having their little house party she'd still be here!!"

The intensity of the anger pouring out of him was so sudden it surprised even himself. Somewhere in his subconscious, he knew he was losing control, but he didn't care. His heart ached for revenge and, at that moment, he was NOT going to be pushed around any more. In fact, he was about to show all of them just how ready he was to push back...

"You fucking better hope they don't touch her." he said, pointing a finger at Dex.

"Don't threaten me homey." Dex responded firmly.

"I aint your fucking homey alright."

"Mark, calm down." Robert said, reaching slowly for his arm.

"Fuck that!" he yelled, snatching his arm away from Robert and immediately turning his focus back to Dex. "Lemme tell you something BOY. Anything happens to her... ANYTHING...and I will string your little black ass up myself."

Dex stood up quickly and removed his jacket. He had a few anger issues of his own and would be more than happy to take his frustrations out on this dudes face.

"Dexter honey, just leave it alone." Toshia cautioned as she stood up to restrain him.

"I aint gonna be too many more BOYS tonight." Dex said, keeping his focus squarely on Mark.

"You'll be what I tell you to be…nigger"

Almost before Mark could get the word fully out of his mouth, Dex snatched his arm away from his sister and lunged at him. Mark reached back to throw a punch but Robert shoved the heel of his boot into the back of his knee, sending him sprawling awkwardly to the floor. He was completely defenseless but, fortunately for him, Walter, who had gotten into position as soon as Mark started threatening the kid, was able to grab Dex around the waist and spin him back against the sofa before he could reach him.

Mark, crazy with rage now, quickly shifted onto his knees and charged toward the sofa from a three-point stance. By his second step however, Robert had grabbed his jacket and, using his momentum against him, pulled him back to the ground onto his side. Before he had a chance to react again he found himself being lifted up off the ground and thrown violently against the far wall, closest to the door. The force of his impact against the wall sent a sharp pain up his spine and slammed the back of his head into the concrete.

Robert pinned him firmly against the wall but, even though he was still dazed from hitting the back of his head, he quickly began struggling mightily to get away. He no longer had a defined target for his anger. The thirst for blood overwhelmed and poured out of him uncontrollably, causing him to lash out wildly in every direction. He wanted, no he NEEDED to kill someone, anyone. It no longer mattered who or why. He just needed for someone, EVERYONE, to lose what he had lost; to feel what he was feeling. He let out a loud, primal scream as he continued fighting until his muscles betrayed him and his body suddenly went limp.

The weight of yet another failure weighed so heavily on him that he was physically unable to stand. Robert, who had been holding him back, was now holding him up when he opened his eyes to see everyone staring silently at him. Only they didn't have the same loathsome looks on their faces from before. This was something different. They felt sorry for him.

"You need to calm down." Robert said gently.

"Don't tell me what to do."

In truth, he had barely heard what Robert said. They were less than six inches apart yet his voice sounded as if it came from somewhere off in the distance. He closed his eyes and tried to clear his head but could still feel their eyes burning into his skin. It was as if they were all trying to look, not at him, but through him. As much as he wanted to hide it, he knew they could now see his weakness. He felt their judgments. He internalized them. And he hated them for it.

"You're acting crazy!" Robert responded harshly, the words snapping him back into the present. He opened his eyes to meet his fathers stare and was immediately reminded of something else that had been taken from him. Only this had nothing to do with any terrorist.

"Well I'm sorry I'm not measuring up to your lofty freakin standards but we're talking about my WIFE!!!"

"For all we know, Amber is fine!" Robert replied, feeling like he might finally be getting through to him. "Do something stupid and you could be the one to get her killed…"

"Well what if you're wrong huh?" Mark asked through yet more tears. "What if she's already…" his voice tapered off at the end as he couldn't bring himself to say the word.

"Then there's nothing you can do about it…" Robert replied softly.

"I swear on my mother," Mark responded, tearfully succumbing to every emotion he was experiencing. "if it's the last thing I do, I will kill every one of them."

And with that he collapsed into Robert's arms and cried. There was as much desperation as rage in his words now, and Robert got the sense he was reaching out. He held him tightly as wave upon wave of despair poured out of his son. He could see in his eyes that he was carrying the unbearable weight of responsibility for not being able to protect his wife and had convinced himself that he was weak; that he was a coward.

But there was only one coward in this room, Robert knew. Only one person who ran from his responsibilities and abandoned his son rather than man up and face the consequences for lies he told himself and so many others. It was his failure that robbed his son of an alternate place of safety far removed from the dark and lonely island he had come to know so well. If Mark Cohen had no idea what it meant to be a man or how to protect his family, there was only one person to blame.

His heart felt like it was literally breaking apart as he thought back on the magnitude of his mistakes. Nothing he had accomplished or gained in his life meant anything because he had failed at the most fundamental responsibility for any man. He had failed his son and was now face to face with the consequences.

He cursed inwardly at how utterly powerless he felt to fix any of the things he had broken all those years ago. The only thing he could do now was comfort his child, 20 years too late, as he cried. That and pray he would make it through this night alive. He held him tightly as he cried and was so lost in thought he never even noticed his own tears…

"Don't touch me." Mark said suddenly, pushing Robert away as if waking up from a bad dream.

The suddenness of Mark's push caught Robert so off guard that he responded reflexively with words he wanted to take back almost as soon as he heard them coming out of his mouth.

"Dammit Mark, I'm your father."

The audacity of what he just heard almost made him laugh out loud. He glared angrily at Robert for a long moment without saying anything. Finally Robert spoke up, feeling the need to explain what he meant.

"Mark, I'm just saying I'm…"

"You're a faggot." he interrupted firmly, this time with no emotion whatsoever. "Why don't you go back over there with the rest of the animals."

The words hurt more than he expected. Robert backed away and sat down, leaving Mark standing by himself close to the door. He leaned forward and rested his head in his hands, feeling completely defeated as he looked back over at his son standing alone. He rubbed his eyes, looked to the floor and sighed deeply when, suddenly, his head snapped back up. His eyes sharpened as he quickly scanned the area around where Mark was standing. Something was wrong...

His eyes stopped scanning and focused in on the door… which had been cracked open.

CHAPTER TWELVE

Mark!" he shouted, standing up out of his seat, but he was too late. By the time he was fully on his feet, the door swung open and the same four gunmen from before entered with weapons at their shoulders.

Mark had no chance to react before Omer had a handgun pressed firmly into his forehead and had backed him up against the wall. The others retreated into the corner again, where they were held by two more men with rifles. Robert nervously stood his ground in the center of the room, unwilling to abandon his son.

"Your time has come my friend." Omer said ominously, staring directly into his captive's eyes as if he wanted to basque in the fear he and his partners were creating.

Mark, for all of his grandiose thoughts of how he would handle himself in the wake of them taking his wife, began shaking uncontrollably. If they had stayed true to form and crashed through the door violently, he may have had more of an opportunity to react or at least steel himself for what was about to go down. But this time there was no shock and awe associated with their entrance. They simply opened the door and walked in, leaving no doubt in anyone's mind who was in control…

"What do you want?" Robert demanded, his voice shaky as he eyeballed the bastard holding a gun to his sons head.

"I'm not talking to you." Omer said calmly. He didn't need to raise his voice. His point was made simply by pushing his gun harder into Mark's head.

"I'm in charge here dammit!" Robert pressed loudly.

"No!" Omer screamed suddenly then lowered his gun and delivered a perfectly placed knee to Mark's kidney. He wheeled around and looked at Robert directly. "I am in charge."

The force of the blow sent Mark to the ground writhing in pain. Omer turned back around, stood over him, chambered a round and aimed his gun directly into his chest.

"No no no!! PLEASE!" Robert cried out desperately, his head spinning in search of a way to stop what was about to happen. After a long moment he realized there was only one thing left to say.

"Take me."

"What?!" Toshia and Dex reacted simultaneously, not believing what they just heard.

Their sudden outburst seemed to startle the gunman closest to them. "Stay the fuck back!" he shouted as he aggressively stepped towards the group. Walter noticed his hands were slightly trembling. He quickly pulled Dex and Toshia back behind him and moved everyone even further back into the corner. His heart was beating so fast he felt light headed but he had maintained enough composure to realize these guys were pretty much focused on the drama across the room. As long as the rest of them stayed calm, they might be ok...for now.

"He's my son goddammit!" Robert pleaded urgently, his voice was shaking horribly. "I am in charge here. Let him go and take me...please." His voice trailed off to almost a whisper at the end as he voluntarily sunk to his knees.

"What the fuck are you doing?!" Mark asked Robert nervously when he saw Omer look over at him as if he was considering his request.

"I will go with you" Robert said submissively, ignoring Mark and keeping his focus solely on the guy with the gun. It killed him to bow down before what he considered to be little more than a well armed street gang, but he knew he had no choice. If he wanted save his son, this is the only card he had to play.

There was a long moment of silence while Omer considered his next move when suddenly, he turned back to Mark, grabbed him by the shirt and pulled him up off the ground. He slammed him violently back against the wall, lowered his weapon and leaned in close enough to whisper in his ear.

"I want you to decide." he said softly so that only Mark would hear. "Either you or your father must come with me."

And with that he stepped back and raised his gun again to Mark's forehead. "Decide!" he demanded as he placed his gloved hand on the trigger.

The dead, still air in the room was heavy as Mark stood there,   eyes closed and his entire body trembling uncontrollably. From where he was standing he could have seen Robert on the ground behind where Omer was standing but he couldn't bring himself to look. The truth is there was nothing left to decide. He just had to bring himself to say the words...

"That faggot aint my father." he mumbled weakly, almost imperceptibly. His mouth was so dry he could barely speak.

Omer smiled at him and leaned in close again. This time he didn't whisper as he fully intended for everyone else to hear what he had to say.

"The frailty of your faith is your greatest weakness. And it is this weakness that serves our greatest purpose..."

"What purpose?!" Toshia cried out from behind Walter as one of the goons pulled Robert to his feet. "Why are you doing this?!"

Omer turned away from Mark and stepped toward the corner. "Our purpose is victory. And our victory is death." he announced ominously then paused to let his words sink in. He turned back to face Mark, who was leaning limply against the wall, completely defeated. "Remember it is YOU who serves our greatest purpose. By god's grace your time will come soon."

With that, he unceremoniously walked out the door, followed by Robert, who was being dragged at gunpoint by two of his men. They walked directly past Mark, who closed his eyes and turned his head to the side rather than risk eye contact with his father. When they were gone, the final gunman backed away from the group in the corner and calmly left, slamming the door behind him.

CHAPTER FOURTEEN

Eleodora Gonzalez always hated the cold and living in Philadelphia for so many years had done nothing to help her get acclimated. In fact, she wanted to move to Florida a year ago but when Lena was accepted to The Philadelphia Arts Academy, they decided to stay until she graduated. For a fleeting moment, she thought about where they might be right now if she had stuck to her plan and moved to Miami but quickly shook that off and reminded herself to stay in the present.

Unfortunately for her, the present temperature in the room had dipped low enough that she could now see her breath start to fog. Of course it didn't help that she hadn't moved a muscle in close to 30 minutes, but that wasn't going to change anytime soon...

Even though her back was aching from sitting in the same position for so long, she dared not move lest she risk waking up her daughter, who had mercifully fallen asleep about 20 to 25 minutes ago. Lena had started shivering when she fell asleep, which was unusual considering she normally dealt very well with the cold. Then again, her trembling probably had as much to do with what was happening to them as it did the temperature in the room.

Whatever Eleodora thought of Robert, she knew seeing an authority figure taken away like that had to be an incredibly difficult thing for any young person to process. Like most parents, she would have given anything to shield her child from such ugliness but the circumstances of this evening had made that impossible. The truth was, she could no longer protect Lena from certain realities. Now she would have to help her cope.

She managed to find an old curtain to use as a blanket and checked to make sure her baby was completely covered before scanning the room to check on everyone else. She obviously didn't know them very well but that didn't stop her from caring. She looked around and saw everyone resting quietly, sort of huddled together in pairs. Except for Mark of course, who was sitting alone by the wall close to the door.

She closed her eyes and quickly found her mind racing, desperately wanting to make sense of what was happening. Obviously they were being held hostage but none of them had any idea why or what, if anything, was being done to help them. Their cell phones had been taken, they were in a basement with no windows and none of them wore a watch so, not only were they completely cut off from the world, they were quickly losing any sense of time. They were completely at the mercy of these lunatics without even a semblance of control over their own fate, and that, she knew, was the worst part.

She forced her eyes open to stop the negative stream of consciousness from forming in her brain. She had to hold it together and focusing on the negative would not help her do that. She had to find a way to stay positive, if not for herself, then for her daughter and the others.

She was honestly proud of herself for the way she'd dealt with everything thus far. If anyone had asked before this night began, she would have been sure she'd have fallen to pieces by now. Yet, through everything, she had absolutely handled herself as well as could be expected and that certainly wasn't because she'd been through anything like this before. To the contrary, her life in Cuba was one of relative comfort.

Eleodora grew up in the Pueblo Nuevo barrio of Cardenas, the maritime port town made famous in America as the childhood home of Elian Gonzalez. Her mother was a school teacher and her father a hotel manager in Varadero, a narrow island that juts into the Straits of Florida on Cuba's northern coast, just to the north of Cardenas. These are two of the most prestigious jobs in the country and afforded them lives that, while certainly not nearly as opulent as what is referred to as middle class in the U.S., were certainly very comfortable and, for the most part, uneventful. No, what gave her the strength to handle this had nothing to do with her childhood home or her parents or anything like that. She drew her strength from the only place she knew to look in times of trouble, her faith.

As she looked around again she felt she could almost hear what the others were thinking, and it saddened her to know most of them hadn't yet discovered what she knew to be true. She knew they were each, in their own way, praying for a miracle. She also knew they would most likely be left disappointed.

Not that she didn't have hope they would make it out of this ok, because she did. Its just that common sense told her things were likely to get a lot worse before they got any better. Her faith didn't shield her from negative thoughts or from being afraid; those things were simple human nature. Her faith let her know she'd be able to stand strong in the face of any adversity, and she could know this because she knew she wouldn't be standing alone.

She first developed a relationship with god as a teenager and had held tightly onto it ever since. It was this maturity that allowed her to be secure enough in her faith to accept that God didn't fly around the sky like some comic book hero, swooping in to save the day at the last minute. Yes, the God she knew had overcome the powers of sin and death but that didn't mean he prevented bad things from happening. In her faith, she knew God grieved with her at the tragedies of her life and would be right beside her through this as he had been through so many other difficult times.

Immediately after the gunmen left the last time, she gathered everyone into a sort of ad-hoc prayer circle.

"Be strong and courageous. Do not be afraid or terrified because of them, for the Lord your God goes with you; he will never leave you nor forsake you."

She recited Deuteronomy chapter 31, verse 6 from memory three times before allowing the room to fall silent so that they could each speak to god in their own way. She knew this was the only way for them to possibly find some measure of peace. She even reached out to Mark who, of course, ignored her and slumped to the floor where he barely moved or made a sound sense.

If she was dealing with this whole thing the best, there was no question who was having the toughest time, but that wasn't a surprise to Eleodora. Without faith, there was no way for anyone to stand up under this kind of pressure and that young man was extremely lacking in the faith department.

To be fair though, outside of her short prayer, no one had done much moving or talking since they took Robert away. This moved the room beyond simple silence and allowed it to become filled with an almost eerie sense of stillness. Robert was the one other person who seemed equipped to handle this kind of situation and him not being there left everyone, including her, feeling a little more vulnerable. He had sort of taken on the role of protector from the very beginning and, just by his presence, made them all feel a little safer. Now he was gone and, as much as she didn't want to admit it, seeing him taken away had changed things.

As horrifying as the scene with Amber was, and Eleodora was certain she would hear those screams every night for the rest of her life, the sheer adrenaline of the moment carried her, and the others, through it. Taking Robert away, however, had the exact opposite effect. Having him dragged off at gunpoint drained some life out of everyone left behind, especially the children to whom he was as much a father figure as a teacher.

The extreme irony of that thought hit her immediately. The same man who had stepped up to lead and protect a room full of virtual strangers in the face of mortal danger had abandoned his child for, as far as she could tell, fear of being called a name. She knew it was not her place to judge but, considering everything they had learned about the man, judgment from somewhere certainly seemed in order. A part of her wanted to give him the benefit of the doubt because he genuinely seemed like a good man. But a larger part of her, the maternal part, found herself looking down at Lena and could not conceive any scenario where she would abandon her child, nor did she even want to try and understand how someone else could abandon theirs.

She closed her eyes and breathed deeply, trying to clear her head. She was losing focus. Her main priority, her only priority right now, needed to be protecting the young girl whose head was resting peacefully in her lap. Nothing else mattered…not even close.

CHAPTER FIFTEEN

W hat are you thinking?"

Lena wasn't actually sleeping after all. She had just closed her eyes, hoping to forget where she was for a few minutes. When that didn't work, she opened them to find her mother staring down at the floor in front of where they were sitting.

"I'm sorry?"

"You looked like you were a million miles away." Lena smiled weakly. "Where were you?"

"I was right here baby."

"Yeah, but what were you thinking about?"

"I don't know; a lot of things."

"Like what?" Lena pressed innocently.

"Like how happy I am."

This caught the 15 year old off guard and she pushed herself up off of her mothers lap so that she could look at her in the eye. "Happy?" she said skeptically. "Mama come on, how can you be happy now?"

"Because I choose to be." Eleodora answered matter of factly, smiling at her little girl.

"I don't understand."

"I know you don't chica." Eleodora answered, gently stroking her hair. "But one day you will."

There was a long moment of silence between them as she allowed her mother's words to sink in. She wanting to tell her how much she meant to her but, as usual, couldn't find the right words. Anything she could think to say seemed silly and wouldn't come close to communicating how she truly felt.

Frustrated at her lack of eloquence, she pulled her knees into her chest and cuddled up as close to her as she could get. Even at 15 years old and on the verge of womanhood, Lena Gonzalez still felt safest in her mothers arms.

"I hope you will be proud of me one day." she blurted out, almost involuntarily.

"Lena stop it. You know how proud I am of you."

Eleodora looked down at her daughter and saw that she had started to cry again. "What is it Chica?" she asked, knowing what the answer was. She wiped the tears from her daughters face and patiently waited for her to respond.

"Mama, I'm scared." Lena said finally, her voice shaking but still loud enough for everyone to hear.

"I know you are." Eleodora answered quickly. "This is a good thing."

"But I don't understand."

"We are all afraid, but being afraid is not what matters." she explained calmly. "It's the choices we make when we are afraid that matter most."

"It is in a time of crisis that each man shall show his true self" Walter offered from across the room.

"Get your philosophy on big dawg, I aint mad at you."

Hearing Dexter's voice seemed to breathe some life back into the room. His youthful energy had been a very welcome distraction earlier but, after seeing Robert taken away, he'd just been sitting silently with Toshia on the sofa. It was obvious that losing Robert hit him even harder than the others but, hopefully, he was starting to bounce back. A little taste of his youthful spirit was exactly what they needed.

"Hey Mrs. Gonzalez." he went on softly. "What kind of music y'all be listening to in Cuba?"

"All kinds."

"Y'all listen to that salsa stuff don't you?"

"Yes but there are other kinds of music as well."

"Do you miss home?" Lisa asked tiredly, wanting to join the conversation and take her mind off everything else.

"Only the people." Eleodora answered honestly. "At home, when you have a problem, everyone helps you. America is not like that."

"I don't know about that." Lisa replied, slightly defensive. "I think it depends where you live."

"What's that supposed to mean?" Walter asked, out of nowhere.

"Umm, I don't know." Lisa replied hesitantly, caught slightly off guard by the tone of his question. "I guess I mean this is a big country with a lot of people and I'm sure there are plenty of places with as strong a sense of community as you can find anywhere else."

"Can you name one?"

"I'm sorry," she answered awkwardly, "I didn't know I was on trial."

"Nobody's putting you on trial Lisa, but if you're going to make a statement like that you should be willing to defend your words."

"What is your problem?" she shot back angrily, not appreciating being put on the spot. "I know we have more than our share of assholes in this country Walter, but you know as well as I do there are assholes everywhere."

"That's a justification." he waved his hand dismissively.

"A justification for what?" she asked sharply, her irritation growing into full blown annoyance with every word out of his

160

mouth. "For allowing people the freedom to be assholes to each other if they choose to be?"

"It's not about the people who are assholes Lisa. It's about your unwillingness to do anything about them."

"And what would you suggest?" she shot back. "That we make showing a lack of compassion for your neighbor illegal?"

"I'd start by standing up for what's right ALL the time. Not just when it's convenient."

"What's right is a system of government where everybody has the freedom to be who and what they want, regardless of what you or I might think of them."

"Ok," he replied sarcastically. "so each man shall have the inalienable right to live in ignorance. I get it."

"Apparently not."

"Sure I do." he went on, his words dripping with condescension. "And of course your so-called system is the best in the history of the world right?"

"My system?" she asked incredulously. "Walter, last time I checked, you lived here too."

"You're right, I do live here. I'm just not living under the same delusion you are."

"And what delusion is that?"

"That you can have a society that accepts ignorance without encouraging more of it."

"Oh come on Walter." she replied in frustration. "You can't control the way people think and you know it. Living with the ignorance of others is a consequence of being free..."

"So," he interrupted. "we should bury our heads in the sand in the name of freedom?"

"Tolerating ignorance is not the same thing as accepting it."

"Lisa, who are you kidding? This society has gone WAY beyond tolerating ignorance. Hell, at this point, we're actually celebrating it."

"You're being dramatic."

"Really? Have you heard of Sarah Palin?"

"Wait a minute." she answered firmly. "Just because you disagree with someone does NOT mean they're ignorant or that they should be silenced. What do you think separates us from them?"

"Them?"

"The bastards who have us locked in this room."

"Personally, I'm more afraid of the tea party."

"You're being silly."

"Really? Well what if I told you there was an entire movement of people living off of government assistance now protesting the government for offering assistance?"

"I wouldn't say they were dangerous." she said calmly. "Misguided maybe, but not dangerous."

"Well what happens when these same, misguided people go on TV and shamelessly yearn for the 'good old days', back when real Americans had real American values'."

"And? If that's how they feel, what's wrong with that?"

"Depends how far back you wanna go doesn't it? Back when you didn't have the right to vote? Not far enough? Ok, how about back to when people who look like me had to ride in the back of the bus? Hell, let's just put the coloreds back in chains."

"Walter stop it. You're being ridiculous."

"Ignorance is not some accident of nature, Lisa. It is a failure of society. AND, it is a far bigger threat to your perfect system than any idiot with a gun."

"So I suppose you'd rather live under sharia law than with the ignorance of other mere mortals less enlightened than you?"

"This isn't about me." he said, shaking his head slowly. "You don't get it."

"Oh I absolutely get it." she answered quickly. "But I'm not about to apologize for having the freedom to be who and what I want, even if who I am is not who YOU, the almighty Walter, thinks I should be."

"Well, I'm not the one you need to be worried about." he answered softly, frustrated by his inability to make her understand.

Eleodora was disappointed, but not surprised, by what she was hearing. She had come to know Americans as something akin to spoiled children, unable or unwilling to objectively self reflect. They took any criticism, no matter how small, as an affront to their standing in the world and considered it to be blatantly disrespectful of all the good things they had done.

What she would never understand was how they couldn't see what was happening right in front of them. Their great kingdom was literally crumbling underneath the weight of an increasingly distracted, under-educated and apathetic population whose sole priority, it often seemed, was their own comfort.

If history had taught the world anything, it's that the fall of an empire begins right around the time that standard of living becomes the organizing principle of their society. This was true for ancient Rome 600 years ago and it was true for the United states of America today. Only, for some reason, they couldn't see it.

"So," she began, knowing it was pointless to argue but wanting to try anyway. "You truly believe you have more freedom than anywhere else in the world?"

"Yes ma'am I do."

"And your freedom includes the freedom to hate?"

"Yes it does." Lisa responded unapologetically. "You will never be able to legislate ignorance or hatred out of the world and you know what? That's the way it should be. Freedom is rarely pretty and it is never convenient..."

"Nice platitude." Walter interrupted. "Unfortunately it doesn't do much for the people being hated. "

Now Lisa was feeling attacked and it was pissing her off.

"Everybody has to find their own path and experience life in their own way Walter." she said harshly, not willing to back down. "If that means you have to live with the ignorance of others, then so be it. It absolutely beats the alternative and you know it."

Walter shook his head. They had been through this debate enough times over the course of their relationship that her views didn't exactly come as a surprise. Still, he assumed this particular situation would have helped her see things a little differently. "So," he said calmly. "We all go on with our lives free to hate whomever we want?"

"Or love whomever we want." she responded smugly. "And I never said we were perfect either. I'd be the first to admit we're far from it; but I do believe our system is FAR better than any other, and if given the choice between being free to do and think whatever I want or having the government try and legislate the way people interact with each other, I choose freedom every time."

"You really believe this?" Eleodora asked.

"Yes I do." she replied confidently. "Are there some negative consequences that come along with our system of government? Of course, but at the end of the day we have our freedom, and again, that is what separates us from them."

Lisa was especially satisfied with herself for successfully making her point without becoming overly emotional. What's more, she genuinely believed everything she'd just said.

"You call this freedom?"

Toshia wasn't purposely trying to be sarcastic. She was just having a hard time removing herself from the here and now of their situation and hearing anyone talk about 'freedom' right now seemed insane.

"Why do you think we're here Toshia?" Lisa asked.

"Because there's a crazy man and a bunch of his friends outside that door with guns ready to shoot us?"

"They are out there because they hate us. And they hate us because our freedom is a threat to them."

"Lisa, I'm sorry." Walter said harshly. "But you can't seriously believe what you just said."

"I absolutely believe it" she responded pointedly.

"How is being free a threat to anybody?"

Dex's question was a good one, Lisa thought to herself. Walter's attitude notwithstanding, she was allowing herself to become lost in this conversation, and found herself enjoying it. It made her feel like she was back in college and having Dex join the discussion shifted her into full-on teacher mode.

"Think about it Dex." she responded patiently. "In a culture where honor killings and gender mutilation still take place, our form of equality and openness can easily be seen as a threat…"

"Gender mutilation?" Lena inquired innocently.

"Female circumcision." Walter answered. "The removal of the clitoris."

"Oh hell no!"

"It's true Dex." Lisa replied. "They believe that eliminating sexual pleasure, reduces the chance of a woman having sex outside of marriage…"

"SEE!" he interrupted, excitedly jumping up out of his seat. "That's what I was tellin y'all before. Them niggers over there is all pent up and aint got no release and…"

"DEXTER!"

He was used to getting yelled at but having Lisa, Toshia AND Eleodora jumping down his throat at the same time was a bit much.

"I'm just saying." he responded, quietly sitting back down.

"I'm sorry Dex." Lisa went on, pressing her point. "That is not what this is about. They hate us because of our freedom, not because they don't get laid."

"That is nonsense."

"It's the truth." Lisa responded, glaring at Eleodora, who was starting to get on her nerves almost as much as Walter.

"No that cannot be true."

"Well, I'm sorry ma'am but I believe that it is."

"How can it be," Eleodora continued. "when you are not free?"

"Excuse me?"

"You are not free."

"I understand we have our issues," Lisa said defensively. "but we are still the freest, most open society on earth."

"Just because you're not in chains does not mean you are free...there are many forms of slavery."

"How can you, of all people, say this country isn't free?!"

"I know what I see."

Lisa could see, instantly, that she wasn't going to be able to get through to Eleodora. "You obviously don't know very much about your new home." she responded, hoping to end the conversation and move on.

"I know this freedom you speak of so fondly is just a dream." Eleodora said quickly, not willing to let it go. "You would see it too if you weren't blinded by this child-like need to constantly elevate yourselves above the rest of the world."

"There is nothing wrong with being proud of where you come from."

"Yes but it would be nice if you actually KNEW where it is you came from." Eleodora responded forcefully, shaking her head in disgust. "Americans...True, you are rich and powerful but that's ALL you are. You define yourselves based on things you have and on what you've achieved instead of who you are inside. This is your greatest failing. You complain of corruption in your government but you do not find the courage to change it too much or too quickly because, lord forbid, you might miss your opportunity to achieve your great American myth…"

"What myth?"

"Abundance!" Eleodora shouted angrily. "The chance to have far more than you could ever need! This is how you've defined your culture and this is how you teach your children to define themselves...based on what they have instead of who they are inside."

"But mama," Lena interrupted shyly. "Why would that make anyone want to kill us?"

"It's about control." Walter answered for her.

"Control how?" Toshia asked.

"Listen," he began patiently. "America's number one export is our popular culture. In this way, we are constantly expanding our sphere of influence around the world."

"And?"

"Well not everyone is in love with our system of government or our lifestyle Toshia. Some people might be threatened by it while others just resent the intrusion. Either way, this constant desire to spread our way of doing things throughout the rest of the world rubs a lot of people the wrong way."

"It's more than that." Eleodora corrected. "There are a lot of people who see this culture as poisonous and want nothing to do with it. What would you do if someone came into your home and tried to feed poison to your family? You would fight them right?"

"Wait a minute." Toshia stood up off the sofa, not believing what she was hearing. "I KNOW damn well you're not saying we're no better than the animals that have us locked up in here?!"

"Look," Walter replied calmly, wanting to methodically make his case without getting sidetracked into an argument he knew he couldn't win. "Does it really matter who's better or worse if the end result is the same for everybody?"

"The same how?"

"We live in fear of a bomb being planted on a plane or some idiot blowing himself up in a crowded room. They live in fear of cruise missiles and drone attacks. The common theme for both sides is that we all end up living in fear of each other."

"Well, personally, I think it makes sense to be afraid of someone who has made it their mission in life to kill you."

"That sounds good Toshia. Unfortunately, if you're afraid of someone it makes it a whole lot easier to hate them."

"Why shouldn't I hate them?!" she responded angrily. "That bastard put a gun in my brothers face and according to you two he did it because he doesn't like MTV! I'm sorry Walter but that's just fucking stupid."

"Arrogance prevents you from seeing a bigger picture." Eleodora offered gently

Toshia didn't appreciate being talked down to, especially by someone who had apparently lost her mind. "So," she replied angrily "we're arrogant if we don't think reality TV is as dangerous as a man with a bomb?! Y'all need to go somewhere with that bullshit."

It wasn't so much what she said as how she said it. The raw, almost primal, anger in her voice let Walter know he was having the exact argument he had been trying to avoid. It was one thing to debate this kind of thing in the teachers lounge amongst his, mostly liberal, colleagues. It was another thing entirely to try and convince a room full of hostages to take a more nuanced view of the world.

At this point, he was ready to let it go and move on. "I get what you're saying Toshia. Believe me I do. I just...I dunno...I think maybe, we have a tendency to oversimplify things sometimes and..."

"Seems simple enough to me." Dex interrupted suddenly.

"Really?" Walter asked, still hoping to change the tone of the conversation. "Tell me what you mean."

"They tryin to kill us so we gotta kill them first. I aint sayin who's right or wrong because I don't care who's right or wrong. All I know is, if it comes down to them or me, I choose them."

"And I can't argue with that. I'm just saying that when you're not in the heat of the situation like this that maybe, you might benefit from looking at things a little differently."

"OH MY GOD! Do you just like hearing yourself talk?!"

CHAPTER SIXTEEN

They had almost forgotten he was there, which was understandable considering he hadn't moved or made a sound since they took his father away. Walter had assumed he was asleep, or in a coma, either of which would have been ok with him. He was just happy he didn't have to deal with the asshole anymore...until now.

For his part, Mark had been about as far from asleep as you could get. He was fully conscious and had been listening to this oversized idiot flex his brain cells for as long as he could without throwing up. He tried to tell himself to ignore it and not get involved but this asshole was really starting to piss him off.

"Listen," he said finally, directing all of his anger towards Walter. "I know you've read a few books and now you need to show everybody you're the smartest guy in the room. But seriously, you really do sound like a freaking idiot."

"I wouldn't expect you to understand."

"And you'd be right." Mark replied sharply. "I'm not fluent in dumb-ass."

That amused Dex a little, who had to try hard not to laugh. After all, he still couldn't stand the dude. Unfortunately the harder he tried not to, the more he found himself wanting to. Eventually, he couldn't fight it anymore...

"Sorry big dawg." he said sincerely. "But that was kinda funny."

"Don't worry about it Dex." Walter said quietly. "It's easy to be funny when you walk around every day completely oblivious to what's going on around you."

"You don't know a damn thing about me or what I do every day."

"I know you're so lost you're pathetic." Walter replied angrily, trying to remain composed even though it annoyed the hell out of him to see Dex laughing at anything Mark had to say.

"I'm lost?! Ha! You gotta be freaking kidding me."

"Nope, dead serious." Walter answered matter-of-factly. "You'll never understand because you're pretty much the dumbest person I've ever met."

"Well, you know who else doesn't understand?" Mark responded, undeterred. "The guys with the guns. So you can talk this pacifist bullshit until you're blue in the face but it won't change the fact that the kid is right. Nobody, I repeat, NOBODY gives a damn about some fake philosophy you looked up on the internet. The assholes who locked us up in here only understand one, VERY SIMPLE, language."

"It only seems simple to you because everything you've ever been taught about your own history is designed to make it seem that way."

"Ok," Mark replied, after a brief pause. "Does anybody else here know what the fuck he's talking about?"

"I'm sorry but you losin me too big dawg."

"There are dots here to be connected Dex." Walter suggested patiently. "You just have to be able to see more than two feet in front of your face connect them."

"And I suppose you have it all figured out huh?" Mark laughed sarcastically

"Look Dex," Walter went on, ignoring Mark. "Written history is basically a one-sided account of previous conflicts, mostly told from the perspective of the winners. As time goes on and these stories are repeated over and over, they eventually become accepted as fact and the truth, your real history, is forgotten. And you have heard the saying about people who forget their history right?"

"They end up repeating it."

"Exactly...So if you believe history as it is told to you by others, you will see this as a simple battle of good vs evil."

"And what's wrong with that genius?" Mark interrupted. "Ever heard of keeping things simple?"

"Unfortunately, simple problems tend to lend themselves to equally simplistic solutions. Like, oh I dunno, like let's just kill all the bad guys before they kill us."

"I'm sorry but that sounds like common sense to me." Toshia said in disgust. She was in no mood to hear any of this right now.

"But there is another problem," Eleodora offered. "The rest of the world is not being taught your version of history so their definition of who is good and who is evil is not always the same as yours. So even though you are made to believe everyone you kill is the devil, you must realize the rest of the world doesn't always agree. For them it is not so simple..."

"And," Walter continued. "if your answer is to just kill all of your enemies, you can imagine you're going to have to kill a LOT of people right? Well, unfortunately, the more people you kill, the more enemies you make. The more enemies you have, the more you find yourself becoming isolated. This goes on long enough and, eventually, you find yourself completely isolated. Now, all of a sudden, guess who ends up as the common enemy? The threat against which the rest of the world aligns itself."

"Us." Lena mumbled.

Walter simply nodded and sat down, allowing the silence they had all been so desperately avoiding to slowly overtake the room once again. The passion with which he had made his case surprised him, even though his opinions certainly weren't new. He had debated these issues with his peers many times. The difference now was that, for some reason, it had become extremely important to him to get his point across to this particular group of people. He felt a desperate need to make them understand and carrying that burden had completely drained him emotionally.

He sat back and tried to relax, and could immediately feel reality beginning to seep back into his consciousness. He guessed the same would soon be true for everyone else as well, once the distraction of their debate completely disappeared, but there was nothing he do about that.

The mood in the room had grown decidedly darker over the last 20 minutes or so and he realized that was mostly his doing. Lisa was purposely avoiding eye contact and, as he scanned the others, it seemed like none of them wanted anything to do with him either. He tried to think of something he could say but knew whatever came out of his mouth would only make things worse. So instead, he sat there, kicking himself for ever opening his mouth in the first place.

"So tell me this." Mark spoke up after a long pause. "When they come back, should we just apologize?"

"What?"

"Well, according to you this is all somehow our fault. So I was thinking maybe we should write an apology letter or something."

"Do whatever you want." Walter replied softly, not wanting to start things up again.

"Maybe we should try talking them to death."

It took him a second to realize it was Toshia speaking instead of Mark this time. He looked over and saw her looking down at the ground, lips pursed tightly together, shaking her head slowly. He could see the anger surging inside her and sensed she was having a hard time containing herself.

"All I was trying to say," he began apologetically. "was that we could benefit from taking a fresh, objective look at our own history and the way we interact with the rest of the..."

"Walter," Lisa interrupted harshly. "Do you seriously think there is any justification for killing innocent people?"

"What?! No, of course not!" he replied defensively. "But it's not treasonous or unpatriotic to self reflect and maybe try and get a fresh perspective on the problem either. If we're interested in winning we can't allow ourselves to be completely naive"

"Since when is maintaining moral clarity naive?" she pressed angrily.

"Since when can you have moral clarity without honesty?!" he replied forcefully. "Do you seriously believe we are innocent victims in this thing?"

"YES!" she screamed at the top of her lungs. "I bought tickets to see a show, not to be shot at and locked in a goddamn room!!" She stood, picked up the closest thing she could find, a small glass picture frame, and threw it hard against the wall, shattering it into a million pieces. Walter saw that she was shaking, but not with fear this time. She was seething with anger and he could tell she was ready to explode.

"Look," he said calmly, trying to settle her down. "You're missing my point..."

"Everybody's missing your point!" Mark interrupted loudly. "You don't debate maniacs with guns alright?! You shoot them before they can shoot you, end of story."

"Oh my god!" Walter exclaimed, trying not to scream. "If you would open your eyes for five fucking seconds you might see that this is a clash of cultures. You can't win it with bullets or bombs."

"So how do we win then?" Mark asked sarcastically. "With flowers and candy?"

"By accepting some responsibility."

"Responsibility for what?!"

"For our lifestyle..."

"Would you PLEASE stop it with this bullshit?!" Lisa exploded at him. She couldn't believe he had the nerve to make excuses for the people doing this to them. "This isn't some stupid fucking grad school lecture, ok?! This is real

179

Walter! We are really locked up in here and we REALLY got shot at in that lobby upstairs! and none of that happened because of our lifestyle!!"

"So you don't think the way we live has any effect on the rest of the world?" he replied, determined to defend himself.

"The way who lives?!" she asked. "Nobody in this country is forced to live a certain way."

"But having the right to make the choice does not eliminate the consequences for having made it. You can't complain about a war for oil in Iraq while you're driving alone in an SUV to a grocery store..."

"Wait a damn minute!" Toshia spoke up loudly. "NOTHING gives ANYBODY the right to hold a gun to my brother's head! We may not be perfect but goddammit neither is anybody else..."

"So because they pointed a gun at your brother, you want to shoot them?"

"You damn right." she replied coldly.

"And what does that get you in the end?"

"I DON'T CARE! If they didn't want to take it there, they shouldn't have started it..."

"But if I were to ask them Toshia, they absolutely believe they are justified in doing what they do based on the things we've done. So all I'm trying to say is that if you could at least understand why they think that way, you'd have a much better opportunity to do the only thing that can stop them from pointing a gun at your brother in the first place."

"Which is what?"

"Stopping the killing." he said as casually as he could. He desperately wanted to make his point but knew he needed to avoid amping up the emotion in the room. "As long as the killing continues, this fight never ends. It doesn't matter who started it or who does the killing or even who gets killed. As long as the killing continues, everyone remains afraid of each other. The longer we're all afraid of each other, the more we learn to hate each other. The more we hate each other, the more justified we feel in killing each other, and the cycle continues..."

"So how do we win if we can't fight back?"

"Here's the thing Dex; when you look at the pictures on the news of the 9/11 hijackers, they are selling the images of these super evil criminal masterminds who were taught from birth to kill Americans right?"

"So what?" Dex replied defiantly. "They attacked us remember? I aint tryin to understand they childhood or nothin like that."

"Ok, but when I see those same images, I see a group of thugs that got lucky. That's it! Not some elite team of criminal superheroes who warrant the shredding of my constitution and the taking away of my freedoms. They're just a group of knuckleheads with a beef and a plan."

"So what's your point?" Toshia asked impatiently

"My point is this idea of simply killing your way to peace will NEVER work. Sure, you can stop the guy from blowing up the building by putting a bullet in his brain. I understand that. But what YOU have to understand is, they only have to be right once. And even a blind man swinging a bat will eventually hit the ball if he keeps swinging long enough. That's what happened on 9/11! They got lucky! Period. And all the bullets and bombs in the world can't prevent somebody from getting lucky every once in awhile...The only way to win is to prevent them from wanting to kill you in the first place."

"This," said Mark emphatically as he stood up off the floor. "is a bunch of BULLSHIT!"

"Only because you are too blind to accept the truth." Eleodora said sternly. "These young men were not born to kill. They were seduced into hating you through your own arrogance and love for violence."

"And," Walter continued her thought. "the lust for revenge that is created by your penchant for violence gives them a purpose in life beyond the pursuit of material wealth, which is something our culture of consumerism and excess doesn't offer. When you put all of this together, you get a VERY different picture of what constitutes a terrorist and the best way to fight terrorism."

"So," Mark began skeptically. "You're saying there is no such thing as evil people in the world then?"

"I'm saying the definition of evil is subjective."

"NO IT'S NOT!" Mark shouted angrily. "You wanna know what evil is, then open that goddamn door and try selling this bullshit to the people on the other side of it!"

Walter sat back down and closed his eyes. Mark was too ignorant to fight with and there was really nothing left to be said anyway. He had done his best to open their eyes and, in the end, he felt like they tuned him out. Now, he wanted to be left alone. He leaned his head back and sighed deeply, too tired to argue anymore.

"Look," Mark said softly, reaching out to everyone else. "There are EVIL people on the other side of that door who want to kill us! They want to put a gun to our heads and KILL US. And the only way to stop them is to kill them first...I'll kill em myself if I have to."

"Which is why it is YOU, who serves their ultimate purpose..." Walter thought to himself, unwilling to say anything more out loud. He was tempted but ultimately knew no one wanted to hear anything else he had to say. What Mark was selling made sense to them so it was pointless to keep fighting it.

He relaxed deeper into his seat, folded his arms across his chest and said nothing. Within seconds, waves of silence began flowing back into the room. Only this time, he welcomed them...

CHAPTER SEVENTEEN

To call it chaos would have been a seriously massive understatement. The phones had been ringing off the hook with publicists pitching various guests, and even quite a few interview requests for the star of the show herself. There were more calls than the three interns, whose job it was to answer them, could handle so they had a few producers pitch in. Even with the extra bodies helping out, hold times were still well over twenty minutes... but no one was complaining.

It wasn't like they were out here by themselves either. Every major news organization in the country had a significant presence in Philadelphia and they had all been running nonstop coverage of the hostage crisis in the city since it began. It's just that none of them had what Street-Wise had...None of them had Marla Cruz.

She was charismatic, she was well-spoken, she could seamlessly read copy from a teleprompter without so much as a cursory review of the material beforehand, and there was no doubting the camera loved her. More important than any of that however, she was a born and bred Boricua from North Philly which gave her a ton of street cred with the locals. While Fox and CNN had the financial backing and the brand recognition and all that; they also had the burden of massive public mistrust of all social institutions, especially the media. Things had gotten to the point where the average guy on the street just assumed he was being lied to whenever he saw something reported on television and since Marla didn't work for a "network" she was instantly considered to be more trustworthy than the talking heads from the majors.

Of course, irrational cynicism was no more a reflection of reality than blind faith but that was somebody else's problem. As far as Marla was concerned perception WAS reality and this hostage thing was like hitting the lottery without buying a ticket. The crisis was WAY beyond the biggest story in Philadelphia. It was the biggest event in the nation and, if the numbers held up, Street-Wise was becoming one of the most watched shows on television. All she ever wanted was the chance to show the world she could hang with the big boys and here it had just fallen into her lap.

Not that she would ever call herself an overnight success. She'd done more than her share of time shopping the clearance rack at Ross...but those days were over. The last episode had a 10.2 rating amongst 18 to 49 year olds, which translated into almost 27 million of the most sought after viewers in the business. Even her agent, who wouldn't return her calls a year ago, couldn't stop gushing and telling her how she was "born to do this." This was absolutely her moment and she was determined to take full advantage of it.

She was in her dressing room, putting the finishing touches on her makeup when someone came barging through the door without knocking. She didn't bother looking up as there was only one person in the building with the balls to walk through her door without an invitation.

"Have you seen this?"

Alex Burnett had been her best friend since they met early in her freshman year at Temple. He was also the senior producer of Street-Wise and was obviously in a panic about something. She braced herself.

"Seen what?"

He handed her a folder with the copy for their next broadcast. It outlined who the guests were, her questions and both her opening and closing statements. She glanced at it, placed it on her dressing table unopened and relaxed into her seat while Margarita finished putting on her face.

"So you're ok with it?"

Alex had a tendency to be dramatic when things didn't go his way so she was trying not to feed into his theatrics. The two of them worked on the student paper for all four years in college and, when he was made editor in chief, he appointed Marla managing editor. They shared an off campus apartment during their senior year and she even went with him when he came out of the closet to his parents. Alex had held her hand through broken hearts, countless drunken nights, and even one brief pregnancy scare. Pretty much everyone left in her inner circle spent as much time kissing her ass as doing their job...not Alex. He was the one person she could count on to speak his mind whether she wanted to hear it or not.

"It's fine, why?"

He picked up the folder and handed it back to her, looking at her expectantly.

"Have you even looked at it?"

"You know you're kinda sexy when you're pissed off."

"We don't have time for jokes," he scolded. "We go live in less than 10 minutes."

"And," she replied as Margarita finished up and began collecting her things. "What's the problem?"

"An Imam Marla? Seriously?"

She'd spent most of the last few hours prepping her wardrobe for the next broadcast. Her director wanted her to review notes on the guests and to approve her own copy prior to finalizing it for the show but she figured that would be a waste of time.

"The guests are fine Alex." she said dismissively, not wanting to admit she hadn't even looked at the list. "Relax."

"The police haven't released any information yet, so how do we even know if this is a muslim thing or not?"

"Seriously Alex?" she laughed. "I guess you think it might be some pissed off white boys from Indiana?"

"I THINK we're supposed to have the facts BEFORE we provide the analysis"

"Here are the facts." she said calmly, not wanting to get too agitated right before she went on the air. "Idiots with guns take over a theater, on the anniversary of 9/11, and hold the entire audience hostage. From there, I think we have the right to make a few assumptions…"

"No actually we don't." he corrected her as he turned to leave the room, knowing he wasn't going to change her mind. He stopped at the door to make one last point before he left. "We're journalists Marla. Our job is to report what we know, not what we suspect."

And with that he was gone…thank god. She loved the guy like a brother but he could be a real pain in the ass when he went off on one of his ethics tangents. She didn't have time to worry about any of that nonsense right now. Her plan was to just get out of the way, let the story take center stage and allow the experts do their thing. If the premise turned out to be wrong, they could deal with that later but, to be honest, she and Alex both knew 90% of the people watching would probably never even know if it was. In this country, in 2013, terrorism meant muslim. Period.

Of course that wasn't entirely fair but nobody was asking her to assess the state of religious prejudice against muslims. Not tonight, not on the anniversary of 9/11, and definitely not when America's extreme paranoia towards this particular religion would appear, to the average Joe on the street, to have been justified.

Alex's livelihood existed behind the camera, so he had the luxury of his principles. Her livelihood depended on the unique connection she had with her audience. She knew they trusted her because she was one of them and, in order to maintain that bond, she had to speak for them, not to them. As long as she was able to 'represent' in that way, they would continue to love her. And as long as they loved her, they would keep watching her...and that was the point. Marla Cruz's job was to make sure every one of her viewers kept watching no matter how mundane the conversation. And to do that, her focus had to be on what they would be focused on, which absolutely wasn't the plight of misunderstood muslims...

After changing her mind enough times to almost drive herself crazy, she finally settled on a brown Salvatore Ferragamo pant suit with a green, Emilio Pucci, silk blouse and an Azza Fahmy necklace and earrings. Of course, Alex thought she should go with something a little more understated but she knew better than that. Opportunity only knocked once in this business and she was about to have 30 million eyes on her. She was going to make damned sure she showed each and every one of them exactly what she was made of…Show time.

The following is a transcript from "Street-Wise with Marla Cruz," September 12, 2013. This copy may not be in its final form and may be updated.

MARLA CRUZ, host: Ladies and gentlemen, welcome to this special edition of Subjective Equivocation. I'm your host Marla Kruse and our discussion will center around religion and violence. An especially relevant topic today, as the hostage crisis at the Annenberg Center for the Arts continues with no end in sight. With us is Ghanim al-Sumahy of The International Islamic Society, Reverend Richard Huey of the New Age Church of Today, and David Pollard of Christiansoftomorrow.com…Gentlemen, thank you for joining us…

ALL: Thanks for having us...

CRUZ: Ghanim, first to you…how do you counteract the negative impression of Islam created by incidents like the one taking place at the Annenberg?

GHANIM: Islam means peace as a way of life for more than 1.4 billion people. There are more than seven million Muslims in the USA alone…One cannot condemn 1.4 billion based on the actions of a few…

DAVID: (Interrupting) "That's just not true… Islam is NOT a religion of peace and the teachings of it's most influential imams and clerics consistently proves that…"

GHANIM: "Allah Almighty honors all the innocent souls that he created. Killing any innocent soul is so hated by Allah Almighty that he considers it as a crime against all of Mankind…In this the teachings of the Qur'an are not very different from the bible…"

DAVID: (Interrupting…) "That is a LIE. As Christians we serve a greater purpose…"

MARLA: "Reverend Huey, let's get you in here…what say you?"

RICHARD: "My views on this topic are well known…"

DAVID: (Interrupting…) "And laughable…"

RICHARD: "Mr. Pollard's assertions of a greater purpose aside, more people have been murdered in the name of god than for any other reason. Assigning blame to an individual or group based on what name they use for god is irrelevant…"

GHANIM: "Marla Cruz if I may…Reverend Hueys argument that religion is bad for society is not true. Islam provides a very effective moral system. Whatever is good for the individual or the society is morally good in Islam. Whatever causes harm is bad…"

DAVID: (Interrupting…) "Killing innocent people is good for society?!"

GHANIM: "As I have said before, these are the actions of a few…"

DAVID: (Interrupting…) "Actions which have yet to be condemned by Muslims…Islam is no more a religion of peace than fascism…Jesus is the true god of love and…"

GHANIM: (Interrupting…) "Have you read the old testament?"

DAVID: "Yes…have you?!"

MARLA: "Reverend Huey what about that? Is Islam a religion of peace?"

RICHARD: "It doesn't matter. The real question is about the role of religion in general, in world conflict. It's not just about Islam…"

DAVID: "We are at war with Islamic fundamentalism! We can't ignore that for the sake of some pointless theoretical discussion…"

RICHARD: (Interrupting…) "Three thousand years of history shows followers of ALL religions violating the sanctity of human life. Christians are certainly not exempt from killing those who do not think as they do…"

MARLA: "What then, do you think is the answer?"

RICHARD: "We need an honest religious discussion. We have to stop pretending that the three religions coming from Abraham have been inherently "good" for humanity…"

GHANIM: "Islam is good for humanity. By setting god's pleasure as the objective of man's life, Islam has furnished the highest possible standard of morality…

Every man should fix his gaze on the love of his fellow-men…"

DAVID: "Five miles from here, we have 100 people being held at gunpoint by lunatics 'fixing their gaze on the love of their fellow men'…"

RICHARD: "World terrorism is not solely the product of Islam, but of the extremism of Judaism and Christianity as well."

DAVID: "The men with the guns aren't Christians…"

RICHARD: "And Nazis weren't Muslims… Look, all I'm saying is that these issues are not unique to any one faith. Self serving interpretations of scripture allow followers of all religions to justify their actions as gods will…"

MARLA: "We have just a little time left…I can allow each of you one final statement. Ghanim, let's start with you…"

GHANIM: "Islam is the religion of peace and the teachings of Islam are based on kindness and consideration of others. A Muslim has to discharge his moral responsibility not only to his family, but to all of mankind. This is the true teaching of Islam. The actions of a few do not represent all Muslims any more than the Ku Klux Klan represents all Christians …My prayers and the prayers of all true Muslims are with the men and women held hostage tonight…"

MARLA: "Reverend Huey…"

RICHARD: "The time has come to question religious scripture and doctrine…not with the mindset of scholars, but as concerned human beings. Let's not forget that all history, religious and otherwise, is written by the winners of the wars and does not necessarily represent the whole truth. Religion is manmade and as such it is inherently flawed. It's purpose is to control and this inevitably leads to extremism, regardless of the faith. It is the same now as always. The men and women at the Annenberg Center for the Arts tonight are only the most recent victims of a conflict as old as human consciousness. Who are we? Until we figure out who we are, we will never know who god is."

MARLA: "David…"

DAVID: "If Islam is truly a religion of mercy, then how do you explain the obvious connection between Islam and terrorism? You don't…As Christians and Americans now is the time to stand for what we believe. Let us not lose moral clarity for there is no moral equivalency to terror. We cannot negotiate with fanatics who aspire to die. We must aid them in their quest. Our way of life and our culture hang in the balance. We have been called to serve a greater purpose…our greatest purpose…we must find the courage to answer this call."

CHAPTER EIGHTEEN

I t had to have been several hours since the last incident and still, sleep managed to elude them. At least for the most part. Every once in awhile someone would succumb to sheer exhaustion only to be unceremoniously jolted back to reality by one of the many terrifying visions of their now 18 hour ordeal..

Lisa shook her head silently at the thought of being locked up for so long. She was beyond exhausted but hers was more of an emotional type fatigue than a physical, '*I need sleep*' kind of thing. She felt like the stress of this night had aged her by ten years and so, even though sleeping was out of the question, the past few hours of peace and quiet was exactly what she needed.

She figured everyone had been sitting silently for, at least, the past two hours only this time they weren't sitting quietly out of fear or shock or anything like that. This time the silence was brought on by the fact that, quite frankly, they had run out of things to say. Whatever novelty existed from being locked in a room full of strangers had long since worn off and now they were just sitting there, staring at the walls and saying nothing so as to avoid getting on each others nerves.

Being left alone for so long did yield one other advantage. The quiet time had allowed a sense of well-being to ease its way back into her mind. The more distance she placed between herself and their last 'visit', the more she could allow herself to believe this nightmare might be closer to its end than it was to its beginning.

Unfortunately several hours of serenity also brought with it a rather intense feeling of boredom. At least before, when they were at each others throats, she wasn't focusing on how isolated they were from the rest of the world. Fighting with Mark and Amber, and even with Walter, gave her something to focus on besides how long she had been without her phone or Facebook or access the internet in general. In todays world, staying connected had become every bit as much of an addiction as smoking or alcoholism and the symptoms of withdrawal, she knew, were strikingly similar. She never considered herself to be addicted to anything but, sitting there with only her own thoughts to entertain her, she had to acknowledge this was the longest she had ever been apart from her iPhone...and it sucked.

She almost laughed out loud at that last thought. Just last year, she started keeping a large tupperware dish on her desk and made her students deposit their cell phones in the dish at the beginning of each class. She could think of countless times she found herself admonishing Walter for texting while they were eating dinner only to find herself sitting here, in legitimate fear for her life, jonesing for her smart phone. Oh well, she thought to herself. At least she, unlike some other people she knew, was self aware enough to recognize her own hypocrisy.

"Hey yo big dawg," Dex said, breaking the hours long silence. "Why you don't wanna get married?"

"Dexter," Toshia scolded. "Mind your business."

"I'm just saying, inquiring minds wanna know."

"I never said I didn't want to get married one day." Walter replied. "I just want to do it right."

"Well, y'all in love aint you?"

"Yes we are, but sometimes..."

"Aww but nothin." Dex interrupted. "Love is where it's at. You got that, you got all you need. That and family..."

"You ever been in love?" Lisa asked tiredly, happily joining a more light hearted exchange.

"Who me?" he answered hesitantly. "Nah, a young brother can't get caught up right now you know what I'm saying?"

"I understand." she replied. "Sometimes you just gotta let a player play."

"Exactly!" he replied excitedly. "See? You know what it is!"

"Ok, mister Player." Toshia said, rolling her eyes. "Settle down."

"All this hatin can't be good for your heart."

"Yeah," she responded playfully. "and you running your mouth aint gonna be good for your health either."

As Toshia playfully slapped her little brother in the head, Lisa looked over, made eye contact with Walter and, without saying anything, the two of them started laughing. She leaned over, rested her head in his lap and, just like that, all was forgiven. He put his arm around her, caressed her shoulder, and she instantly felt safer knowing they were ok. Not that she should have had any doubts. It's not like they never had an argument. In fact, they fought quite a bit, but that never concerned her. She thought it was healthy that they were both so strong-willed and confident enough to speak their minds, even if their opinions didn't always mesh perfectly.

If she learned anything from the failed romances of her past it was that the true test of any relationship, romantic or otherwise, only came once the other person pissed you off. That was when you knew if it was real or not. If you found yourself holding a grudge then, chances are, you weren't all that invested in the first place. Conversely, if you were able to let things go and bounce back from disagreements quickly, then you were probably onto something more real. From the very beginning, she had few doubts about their relationship because, even though there were dozens of times when they literally wanted to strangle each other, neither one of them was capable of staying mad for very long.

What's it like?" Lena asked innocently, interrupting Lisa's train of thought.

"What's what like sweetie?" Lisa responded softly

"Being in love…"

"Oh. Well, in a word? Amazing."

"It's about seeing past what's on the outside." Eleodora offered. "and allowing someone to see you for who you are on the inside as well…"

"Have you been in love mama?"

"I was young once too Chica."

Eleodora couldn't help but smile. Lena had always been very mature for her age but there were still times when her childlike innocence would shine through. These were the moments she would miss the most…

"My mother used to say love is when you care about someone more than yourself." Toshia suggested, her arm draped around her little brothers shoulder.

"When you are young," Eleodora went on, gently stroking Lena's hair. "it is about having butterflies in your stomach and not being able to sleep…"

"It changes?"

"It is more real when you get older. Not as exciting maybe, but more certain. In this way it can be more scary for men than for women."

The last part was intended for Walter, who was still sitting on the couch with Lisa. He could tell she was poking him and thought about letting it go, seeing as things had settled down from before and he wasn't trying to get into another argument. His curiosity got the best of him however and he decided to take the bait.

"Why do you say that?"

"Men define themselves by their women." Eleodora responded. "This is true in every culture."

Ok, I'll take that." he said confidently. "But I hope you're not implying I don't adore Lisa or that I am, in some way, ashamed to be with her."

"Is this not the case?"

"Listen," he replied firmly. "I love Lisa more than I have ever loved any woman and…"

"And yet," she interrupted. "The idea of loving her forever frightens you."

She smiled mischievously, knowing he had walked into her trap. This was what her own mother might call, a teachable moment.

"Listen," she began. "When a man promises to love someone forever, he is accepting a limit on what forever means. He is, in fact, acknowledging his own mortality."

"Like when they say til death do us part at a wedding." Dex offered enthusiastically.

"Exactly," she continued, looking squarely at Walter to make her point. "So you can see how it might be easier to continue without making the promise because, with that promise, you lose your illusion of forever."

"So what's your point?"

"That love, true love, is not something you see in movies or read about in books. Being in love means wanting to grow old together. And you cannot do this until you accept that one day you will, in fact, grow old…"

She studied his reaction and could tell by the look on his face she had effectively made her point. She looked at him closely, patiently waiting until he looked back and made eye contact. When he did, she smiled warmly.

"Even the wisest among us has much to learn…"

The flood of emotion rushing through him at that moment seemingly came out of nowhere and hit him so fast he was having a hard time processing exactly what he was feeling. The dominant side of his brain; the rational side, thought maybe it could be explained away by fatigue, or the pressure of the situation or, more likely, some combination of both. The weaker side of his brain; the emotional side; the side he rarely indulged, instantly knew better.

It wasn't as if he saw the events of his past replaying for him like happens in the movies. This was more like seeing an abstract painting of his entire life begin to crystalize right before his eyes. Unfortunately, the more clarity he gained; the more clearly he was now able to see what had been right in front of him all along...the less he liked what he was seeing.

He found himself staring helplessly at an intricate mosaic made up of each of his goals, as well as his many excuses for not achieving them. It was as if he had been given a Jackson Pollock rendition of his life depicting, in excruciating detail, all of the opportunities and potential lost to procrastination and laziness. Worst of all, he was now face to face with a reality nearly as horrifying as anything that had happened to him that night...his life was passing him by.

He'd literally watched years of his life slip away because nothing was ever good enough for him. He never allowed himself to enjoy anything because he refused to live in any moment he deemed to be less than perfect. It didn't matter what the situation was or how it appeared to anyone else because he had the uncanny ability to pick apart any single moment or event and focus solely on what was missing. He'd spent so much time waiting for the perfect moment or the exact right set of circumstances that, eventually, waiting was all he ever did.

It wasn't often he found himself speechless. His normally nimble brain came up frustratingly short as he searched desperately for the right words to express what he was feeling. Not a single word or phrase in his extensive vocabulary came even remotely close. It took him a minute to realize what he was doing and, in spite of everything, he allowed himself an inward smile. 'old habits...'

"I'm sorry."

"I'm sorry too babe."

He laughed quietly and lifted her up off his lap so he could look her in the eye. "I don't think you understand." he smiled. "I'm sorry for everything."

"Walter, what are you talking about?"

"I've wasted so much time," he began hesitantly, the natural eloquence he'd known for much of his life abandoning him when he needed it most. "I dunno. I guess I had this idea, this fantasy of how my life was supposed to be and I've never been willing to let it go."

"Well I'm sorry you're disappointed." she replied softly, tears welling up in her eyes.

"No no no!" he said in a panic. "you're misunderstanding me."

"I understood you just fine Walter." she said, turning away from him.

"No, that's not what I meant."

"Did you not just tell me you're not happy with the way your life turned out?"

"I meant I'm not happy with the choices I've made."

"Excuse me?" she challenged, wheeling her head around to stare him down. She couldn't believe he was going there but wasn't about to sit there and be disrespected. "You really want to go there right now?"

"Lisa stop." he pleaded sincerely. "You have to let me try and find the right words."

She studied him curiously for a moment. She'd never known him to have even a small problem finding the right words to say anything. She took a breath, forced herself to relax and reached out for his hand. "Just say what's on your mind."

He placed his hands on hers, pulled it to his lips and gently kissed her fingertips. He closed his eyes and sighed deeply, still searching fruitlessly for the right words. "I guess...I dunno...I guess I'm saying I've spent so much time waiting for my life to live up to my own dumb expectations that, somewhere along the line, I stopped living."

"I understand Walter but you shouldn't have to settle..."

"That's just it," he interrupted confidently, relieved to be finally finding some kind of linguistic rhythm. "Whatever ideas I had in my head were formed based on childish bullshit, kinda like a teenage girl trying to live up to some airbrushed image of beauty she sees in a magazine."

She nodded and smiled warmly as she could now begin to see where he was going.

"I couldn't have possibly found the life I was looking for because the life I was looking for doesn't exist in the real world." His words were tinged with enthusiasm as he now knew exactly what he wanted to say. "But here's the thing," he went on, standing up from the sofa.

"Do ya thing big homie!!!"

"SHUT UP!!!!"

The angry chorus of every female voice in the room scared the exuberance, and a few other things, right out of Dex. He promptly sat back down and kept his mouth shut.

Walter now knew he had an audience but it was too late to worry about anything like that. He was determined to finish what he started, even if his heart felt like it might beat right out of his chest.

"I'm such an ass." he laughed nervously.

"I can agree with that." Lisa smiled through her tears. Like everyone else, she now fully understood where this was going, only she was in no hurry for the moment to be over. She was going to savor every minute.

"I've wasted so much time." he continued "Chasing some ridiculous fantasy when my own reality has always been so much better...you know what I'm trying to say?"

"Yeah, I think I get it." she replied, her voice shaking.

"No, I don't think you do." he replied, smiling confidently. He waited a second to let the magnitude of the moment build, then smoothly knelt down onto one knee...

CHAPTER NINETEEN

Will you marry me?"

The words drew an audible gasp from his soon to be fiancé. It didn't matter how many times she'd rehearsed this moment in her head, experiencing it still took her breath away. Her mind was racing so fast she forgot to give an answer.

"Does that mean yes?"

"YES!" she screamed, melting into his arms.

They held onto each other desperately, neither of them wanting the moment to end. They were so caught up together they never noticed applause coming from the others.

"Now we got that outta the way, we got to do the damn thing big dawg!"

"Dex," Walter asked, still in a daze. "What the hell are you talking about?"

"You can't have no wedding without no planner right?"

"I guess." he responded, still confused.

"Well since we don't have one the best man has to do it. And since I'm the only other brother in the room, I guess that makes me the best man, which means I get to throw the wedding!"

"Boy, what are you talking about?" Toshia asked. She broke away from congratulating Lisa in time to overhear the last part of the exchange between Dex and Walter.

"They getting married right?"

"Fool," she laughed loudly. "They aint getting married here!"

"Why not?!" he asked. "Y'all got something better to do?"

"HELL NO!"

Mark had been remarkably silent through the whole proposal thing and would loved nothing more than to have stayed that way. The whole thing seemed obscene to him and he wanted no part of it. Unfortunately, his idiot roommates wouldn't allow him to keep to himself. They actually seemed like they were considering listening to this pain in the ass kid, so he had no choice but to say something.

"This is NOT happening." he said as firmly as he could. "You understand me?"

"Man please," Dex laughed. "You aint the boss of nobody."

"You idiots never learn do you?" Mark replied, standing up to address the entire room."This is not a freaking house party!"

"Nobody said it was."

"But you wanna have a goddamn make believe wedding?! What the hell is wrong with you?!"

He was panicking and everybody could see it; not that he didn't have a point. There was an uncomfortable moment where they all sat there, none of them knowing exactly what to do. Finally, Lisa broke the silence

"Maybe he's right?" she said hesitantly, hating herself for agreeing with him but unable to debate his logic. "Maybe we should just sit tight and ride this thing out."

"Look," Dex offered quickly, seeing he was losing his crowd. "They gonna do what they gonna do. Nothing we do, or don't do, in here is gonna change that."

"Dex has a point too." Walter said quickly, now warming to the idea. "it's not like we're gonna get out of here early for good behavior."

"And they ain't trying to shoot us cause we had some fun neither." Dex continued, driving his point home.

"Oh, that's right." Mark responded sarcastically. "I forgot you guys were experts."

"Nobody's saying they no expert man." Dex replied, displaying an impressive amount of patience in making his case. "But let's keep it real, ain't none of us in here cause we wanna be or cause we did nothin to deserve it.

"So?" Mark pressed impatiently. "What the hell is your point?"

"My point is aint nobody asked to be in here, but we all in here just the same now aint we? And it aint up to you or me or nobody else in this room when or how we gonna get out...but it IS up to us what we do while we waitin."

"You don't poke a sleeping dog man!" Mark pleaded desperately. "if they are leaving us alone, why can't you just sit down and shut up until this is over? Did you forget what happened the last time you tried to have a little fun?"

"Look, I'm sorry they took your girl but they aint do that cause we was dancing. They was gonna do that anyway."

"You willing to bet your life on that?" Mark replied angrily. "Because I'm damn sure not ready to die in here tonight."

"And how is that different than any other day?" Toshia asked. "I mean, when you woke up yesterday I'm sure you were no more ready to die than you were this morning but you still managed to live your life. And you lived it even though you knew it wasn't going to be forever. Maybe you didn't think about it or talk about it, but you still knew it."

"So what! That doesn't mean I wanted to speed things along!"

"But that's what we saying man." Dex replied confidently. "When or how you go out aint always up to you. What IS up to you is how you live while you here. And right now, like it or not, this is it for us. Our world aint out there no more cuz.

Homeboy and his friends put the brakes on that. So, at least for right now, our world is right here in this room and we can make the best of it or we can sit here wasting whatever time we have left cause we scared."

"Oh so now you're not scared?" Mark asked sarcastically

"It's one thing not wanting to die homie." Dex answered. "It's another thing to be too scared to live."

The transformation in Dex was nothing short of amazing, Eleodora thought, although she always suspected he was capable. He was certainly a smart young man and possessed all the traits of a natural leader. His problem was he spent so much time clowning around that his antics masked his potential. Not anymore. This was a young man who was finding his voice...

"I say we go for it." Lisa smiled quietly "Who says we can't have a wedding?"

"HELL NO!" Mark shouted with as much authority as he could muster. It wasn't enough.

"Man please," Dex laughed. "Nobody said your ass was invited no way."

"Do you assholes want to die?!"

Dex shook his head and smiled. This guy didn't know when to quit. "Whatever happened to you getting your Rambo on and killin everybody?"

"Fuck you nigger!"

He said the words with as much venom and hatred as he could find in his heart, then immediately braced himself for the expected reaction; only it never came. The biggest responses he got were from Toshia, who simply rolled here eyes and Walter, who shook his head, laughing at how pathetically unoriginal he was. Their message was clear. His words had lost their effect.

Eleodora couldn't help but smile to herself. She had tuned Mark's nonsense out hours ago but was afraid the others would still allow themselves to be baited. They didn't. Much like Dex had matured right before her eyes, she could see signs of growth in everyone else too. And it wasn't just about ignoring Mark.

Technically, he was right of course. On the surface, it was nothing short of ridiculous for them to be staging a wedding right now and Eleodora knew that. She also recognized something bigger was happening. Something special.

They had been locked in a cold, dark room for hours with no way of escaping and, when given the choice, they collectively, almost instinctively, chose to live in hope. Even Mark's silly provocations, which rattled everyone so badly earlier, could no longer penetrate their collective resolve

214

to own whatever piece of the world was left to them which, as Dex just said, was now this room.

It was as if the right to self determination had been so thoroughly engrained in their thinking that it had become a part of their DNA. They simply weren't going to allow anyone outside of their world to tell them how to live in it. This wasn't about any silly wedding. This was about them standing up for themselves the only way they knew how. This was about them owning their fate. So while she was relieved when they didn't respond to Mark, she felt something else as well. She felt vindicated.

She argued with Lisa earlier that Americans were like petulant teenagers and she firmly believed this to be true. What she didn't say was that the same immaturity that bred arrogance and stubbornness also created in them a childlike optimism and resiliency. As vapid and destructive as the results could sometimes be, theirs was a culture that rejected limits and, much like a child who had not yet learned to accept the boundaries of their potential, they sincerely believed nothing was beyond their reach. This, more than anything else, was why she left her family behind and came here.

What Lisa couldn't bring herself to understand was that Eleodora Gonzalez hadn't left Cuba behind and come to America because of any great longing for the supposed freedoms of her adopted home. Nor was she escaping any kind of dramatic persecution in the home she left behind. She came to this country to give her daughter the one thing you couldn't get anywhere else in the world...The American spirit.

Everyone immediately got busy setting things up. Dex and Walter cleared out a space in the middle of the floor for the ceremony while Lisa and Toshia started digging through the old wardrobe boxes to find something they could use as a dress.

"Mama can I help them?"

"Yes," Eleodora smiled. "Have fun."

From her very first words to this very day, the sound of her baby's voice had always made Eleodora smile. In fact, there were more than a few occasions when it was the only thing that did. This time however, as she watched her go and join the others, Eleodora found herself fighting back tears. There were so many things she wanted to do differently. So many things she wanted to say. She needed more time...unfortunately more time wasn't part of gods plan.

CHAPTER TWENTY

Amazingly, no one reacted at first. They just stared helplessly at the motionless silhouette now standing in the doorway with no idea how long he'd been standing there or why he wasn't moving. What they did know was the fear that had supposedly dissipated over the past several hours had returned suddenly, and with a vengeance.

The room immediately fell silent and they all froze in place. No one wanted to make any sudden movements or do anything that might trigger any kind of unintended reaction. He was the guy with the gun, after all, so they would take their cues from him...And he wasn't moving.

"What's going on?"

The emotionless, almost robotic sound of his voice sent chills through Lisa and she felt herself beginning to hyperventilate. As much as she desperately wanted to stay strong, she knew, in her heart, she didn't have it in her anymore. The physical and emotional strain of their captivity had already taken a horrible toll and now, seeing this monster appear out of nowhere like that, literally made it difficult for her to breath.

"Please let us go." she pleaded through a massive wave of tears that poured out of her involuntarily, as if cued by the sudden appearance of the man to whom she was speaking. "Please don't hurt us anymore." she cried out shakily, hating herself for how pathetic she sounded.

"You sound afraid." responded the voice from the doorway, still not moving.

Mark was the closest to the door but, like everyone else, his brain was slow to catch up to what was happening. Gradually he found his bearings and started backing away. After a few steps, he caught his foot on one of the boxes Dex moved, and stumbled loudly to the ground.

For the next few seconds, it felt like time stopped. No one said anything or made any kind of sound whatsoever. Not a gasp, not a scream; nothing.

This was it. They each held their breath, bracing for what was about to come...only nothing happened. The silhouette remained eerily unfazed, standing as perfectly still as they did.

The stress of standing there like that was excruciating but, when compared to the alternative, it was absolutely the best option they had.

So they stood there, cemented in place, silently praying for a miracle but not taking their eyes off the dark image in the doorway.

Finally, after what seemed like an eternity, Walter composed himself enough to speak.

"What..." he began, trying, unsuccessfully, to steady his voice. "What do you want?"

Ignoring the question, Omer slowly entered the room and walked directly over to where Mark was sitting on the floor. He had a black handgun in his right hand but did not go out of his way to visibly threaten anyone with it. He didn't have to. His point was made by simply allowing it to hang there by his side, like a deadly appendage.

Two more men with rifles entered behind him, only this time they kept their distance and stayed close to the door. Omer stood over Mark, glaring down at him for a long moment before speaking.

"Who's next?"

"What? ...I...I don't understand?" he lied, knowing full well the implication but desperately stalling for time.

"You decide." Omer said forcefully. "Who's going to come with me?"

In a threatening show of force, the two remaining gunmen each chambered a round and raised their rifles to their shoulders, drawing an audible gasp from the rest of the hostages. The tension in the air was suffocating but everyone remained perfectly still, literally paralyzed with fear.

Looking up at his attacker, Mark started shaking uncontrollably, his throbbing heartbeat pulsating deep into his brain. This was a fear like nothing he had ever known and all he wanted at that moment was for it to be over.

But for that to happen he would have to respond to this bastards question with everyone listening. And that mattered to him. Somehow, in spite of everything; even with his body betraying him and on the verge of a nervous breakdown; somehow there were enough remnants of pride left in him to give him pause.

"Go to hell…" he stammered unconvincingly. "You…you can go fuck yourself."

It was complete bullshit. He knew exactly what he needed to do and had every intention of doing it, but that didn't stop him from feigning one last bit of defiance before going there. Omer knew he was full of shit as well.

"Do you think I will not kill you?" he smiled calmly, never raising his gun.

Mark said nothing.

Out of nowhere, Omer reached down with his left hand and slapped Mark hard across the face, knocking his head into the wall behind him. In one continuous motion, he placed the same hand on top of his nine millimeter desert eagle, pulled back the slide and released it.

Mark, still dazed from the blow to his head, immediately recognized the sound of a round being placed in the chamber. He was running out of time...

"I can take one of them or I can take you!" Omer shouted angrily. He was quickly losing patience and started raising his gun to Mark's chest...times up.

"OK OK!" Mark cried out hysterically, raising his hands to indicate he would play along.

"Take him." he said softly, pointing at Walter.

"You fucking asshole!" Lisa screamed, lunging in Marks direction.

Had she stopped to think about it she would have been as surprised as anyone, especially considering less than a minute ago she was on the verge of falling apart. Only she didn't have time to analyze anything right now. She didn't know where she found the strength and didn't care. Walter was her family and threatening him sent her into a seething rage that she didn't feel the need to understand or contain. Maybe it was adrenaline or maybe she had finally snapped. Either way, it didn't matter. The point was, in that instant, she wasn't afraid anymore; far from it. Lisa Woodward was fully prepared to die right there where she stood before she was going to let ANYBODY fuck with her family.

"Lisa stop it!" Walter shouted, trying to snap her out of it while nervously eyeing the two men pointing rifles at them.

"This is some bullshit!" Dex exploded, spurred on by Lisa's outburst.

"You have a problem?" Omer responded, glaring at him angrily over his shoulder.

"Dex," Walter said nervously. "Calm down buddy, ok?"

It was too late for that. Every person has a breaking point and, like Lisa, Dex had reached his.

"NO, damn that!" he shouted defiantly, staring Omer down with as much hatred as he was getting in return. "How come he gets to decide?! Who the hell is he?!"

Omer turned his back to Mark and took a step towards the others.

"Dexter shut up!" Toshia screamed, nervously eyeing the gun in Omer's hand

"I aint goin out like no punk." Dex replied, holding his ground.

"He decides," Omer said ominously. "because I say he does!"

"You know this shit aint right!"

"What do you know about what's right?!"

"Why can't you take him?!"

"Or I could take you."

Omer raised his gun but Dex was unwilling to back down anymore, even as Omer pointed it directly at his head.

"Put down that gun, we'll see who takes who."

"Dexter stop!" Toshia screamed hysterically as Omer calmly placed his index finger on the trigger.

Everyone froze as he steadied his arm and glared hatefully at Dex, his finger resting precariously in place. It took every ounce of inner strength he had not to apply the approximately 4.1 pounds of pressure required to shut this asshole kid up and remind every one of his godless friends who was in charge at the moment. Only he wanted to do more than kill them...he wanted to hurt them.

"Who else?"

His emotionless voice again pierced the silence as his words sent chills up all of their spines. The realization of what was happening made it's way around the room like dominoes falling on a board, hitting each of them like a heavyweight punch in the gut. It took only a second for reality to set in and then they all began chaotically speaking at once.

"Please," Toshia begged. "don't do this..."

"Come on man," Walter chimed in desperately. "it doesn't have to...."

"Please sir," Lena joined the chorus, through a flood of tears. "Please don't..."

"SHUT...UP!!" Omer shouted, losing his temper and waiving his pistol erratically in their direction. "EVERYBODY SHUT THE FUCK UP!!!

When they all stopped talking, he whirled around and pointed the gun at Mark. "WHO ELSE?!?!?"

"I will go." Eleodora volunteered before Mark could answer.

"Mama what are you doing?!" Lena screamed hysterically, throwing herself into her mothers waiting arms.

Eleodora closed her eyes, held her daughter and sighed deeply, the tears she had been fighting now flowing freely. She thought back to every moment of her baby's life, allowing the vivid images in her memory to linger in front of her, building a sort of ethereal portrait of their lives together. They had never been apart from each other and Eleodora had always taken pride in that. She was fond of saying she was the only person Lena had seen every single day of her life. What she was seeing now, is that worked both ways. Since the day her baby girl was born she had ceased to know a world without her in it.

Dear lord please take care of my baby...

She tried opening her eyes but could barely see through the cloud of tears. She was breaking down. Her body was trembling, her heart was beating faster and she felt like she couldn't catch her breath. This was all happening so fast...too fast. She closed her eyes again and tried to quiet her mind.

For God has not given us a spirit of fear, but of power and of love...

She faithfully repeated those words over and over until they began to build a fortress around her heart. She allowed the words to feed and fill her spirit so completely there was no room left for fear or self-doubt. Gradually, she started to settle down and found herself wondering where the time had gone. It seemed like only yesterday, she was holding her baby girl praying to god to watch over her. She remembered how scared she was when she brought her home from the hospital and crying tears of joy when she made her first friend in preschool.

Most of all, she felt overwhelmed by the amount of love that now filled her heart. Through Lena, the lord had blessed her with an opportunity to know unconditional love and that, she knew, was the greatest gift of all.

"It'll be ok chica." she whispered, accepting that gods plan was better than her own. "You have to be strong for me ok?"

Lena wanted to respond but, no matter how hard she tried, words wouldn't come out. She ended up simply nodding through her tears as Eleodora stepped away from their embrace, leaving her to feel truly alone for the first time in her young life.

"Mommy NO!!" she screamed, collapsing hard to the floor. "Please don't leave me!!"

Eleodora turned to go to her but was pulled back by one of the gunman. Seeing this, Toshia rushed over to Lena's side to comfort her. Dex, realizing he had to keep his emotions in check, walked over to Lisa and pulled her away from Walter, who also calmly turned to leave.

"Please," Lisa cried, as her fiancé made his way toward the door. "Don't hurt him."

Both Eleodora and Walter were ushered out of the room by the two men standing by the door, leaving Omer behind, standing beside Mark. He scanned the room and seemed satisfied with the amount of devastation he was leaving behind. As invincible as they once felt, they now knew what it felt like to be utterly powerless. And living with that, he knew, even for a short time, was a far worse fate than any quick death. Nicely done...

He smiled through his mask and placed his left hand on Mark's shoulder. "By gods grace, this will all be over soon."

And just like that, he was gone...

CHAPTER TWENTY ONE

How's it feel?"

"How's what feel?"

"Goin out like a little bitch!"

Dex was seething with anger. He and Toshia were doing the best they could but both Lisa and Lena were pretty much inconsolable at the moment. Meanwhile, this piece of shit looked like he was sitting there peacefully.

The reality was far different of course. In truth Mark was dying inside. He had already watched both his wife AND his father taken away so he didn't feel the need to apologize for anything.

"Could you at least try and speak English?"

"He said you're a fucking coward!!"

Lisa's sudden outburst caught Dex sufficiently off guard that she was able to knock him off balance and get past him. In a flash she was on top of Mark, who was as unprepared for her onslaught as Dex.

She exploded into him with all of her weight, knocking him back into the wall where they fell to the ground. She flailed wildly with both closed fists and open hands, managing to scratch the side of his face, drawing blood. The site of his blood seemed to ignite a primal instinct in her and she found herself subconsciously clawing in the direction of his eyes. Before she could do any real damage, Dex and Toshia pulled her off him.

The sight of him lying there bleeding did nothing to quell the flow of rage pouring out of her. She struggled fiercely to get back at him, kicking and swinging so wildly that she ended up losing balance and falling to the ground, taking both Dex and Toshia with her.

Mark struggled slowly to his feet, still disoriented from this crazy bitches' assault. His entire body already ached from getting slapped around earlier and now his face stung with the pain of the fresh wound. He wiped the blood from his cheek and leaned tiredly against the wall.

"What the fuck is your problem?"

"You are!" Lisa responded immediately, trying again to go after him. This time Dex was prepared and easily held her back.

Seeing her on the ground, fully restrained, gave Mark a sense of security. He settled back against the wall and glared at her spitefully. "Why?" he asked calmly. "Because I didn't save your pet? Trust me, you're better off."

The arrogant, remorseless tone of his voice nearly drove her over the edge. She had never despised another living thing the way she hated this man.

"What the hell is the matter with you?!"

"With me? Nothing," he smiled cockily. "I'm not the one marrying outside my species."

"Could you please drop that bullshit?!" Toshia screamed, having heard enough. "We could all die here and..."

"You think I don't know that?!" he interrupted angrily.

"You don't act like it!" Lena piled on, using her searing hatred for him as fuel to find her voice.

"And what am I supposed to do?!" Mark asked defensively. "Sacrifice myself to save one of you? I don't think so."

"Do you really hate yourself that much?" Lisa asked, shaking her head.

"Save the psychology crap! I'm doing what I have to do to get out of here alive!"

"And to hell with everybody else right?"

"Oh well."

"Is that why you just sat there crying like a little pussy when they took your wife?"

Had Dex said it, no one would have thought much of it. But coming from Lisa, the words had an especially sharp edge to them...and that's exactly what she intended.

Her words cut through him like a knife, mostly because he agreed with them. He knew he had failed to protect his wife and would have to live with that fact for the rest of his life, however long that was.

"There was nothing I could have done about that." he offered unconvincingly.

"You keep telling yourself that." Lisa responded, purposely twisting the knife much as she could. If there was anything like justice in the universe, they would all live long enough to spit on this bastards grave.

"Well," he replied weakly. "Unlike you, I love myself and my race..."

"Dude!" Toshia interrupted loudly. "Would you just shut the hell up!"

"Nobody wants to hear anymore of your bullshit!" Lena screamed.

"Oh really?" he responded angrily. "Well if you're so tired of my bullshit sweetie, maybe I'll do you a favor and send you away next."

His words hung in the air as if suspended in time, sending a uniform chill through the four remaining hostages, who had no idea what to say or how to respond. It was as if their world suddenly stopped rotating, but instead of being thrown forward, they were left frozen awkwardly in place.

The brutal and abrupt descent back into reality would have been devastating enough to their already fragile psyches. But coming from where it did left them feeling as if God himself was punishing them. They sat in stunned silence for long moment before Lisa spoke.

"You," she began venomously. "Are a pathetic, little, man."

"You sure you wanna talk to me like that sweetheart?"

It wasn't bravado this time. Mark had had all he could stand of being pushed around, especially by this collection of genetically damaged half breeds. If they wanted to gang up on him then he was gonna have to do what he had to do. And if that meant accepting a deal with the devil, so be it.

"You are going to rot in hell right next to the bastards doing this."

He shook his head and managed a weak laugh before responding. "Lemme tell you something. I'm locked in a room with a bunch of freaks. My wife is dead and I have a faggot for a father who's probably dead too. Sweetie if this ain't it, I'm sure hell is much better."

Dex had finally heard enough. "I ain't trying to listen to no more of your bullshit!"

"You wanna move to the front of the line nigger?"

"We ain't gotta wait for ol boy to come back." Dex replied, standing up. "We can finish this shit right now."

"You think so?" Mark asked nervously, backing up toward the door.

"Yeah, I think so..." Toshia answered, standing beside her brother.

"Wanna know the difference between you and your friends out there?" Dex asked rhetorically, moving slowly toward Mark. "You ain't got no gun."

CHAPTER TWENTY TWO

The Fountain Restaurant, inside the Four Seasons Hotel, had long been considered one of the premier dining destinations in the city, if not the entire nation. Equal parts romantic and distinguished, the main dining room seduced the senses with the calming glow of soft candlelight while the well trained staff attended to your every need with an almost militaristic precision. From the moment you walked through the door, everything possible was done to prepare your pallet for an absolutely exquisite culinary experience.

Today, however, was not about the food. The refined decor, accented by custom glass artwork and soundproofed walls, created the perfect ambience for something more than sharing a meal. It was also an ideal place to have an intimate conversation...And that's exactly what Marla was going for.

"Everything had to be perfect." she thought to herself as Margarita finished her makeup and left her alone to prepare. They had set up a makeshift dressing room in one of the four, 1100 square foot executive suites located in each corner of the hotel. Each suite came equipped with a full marble bathroom, a 42 inch, wall mounted, plasma television and a view of Logan Circle. The latter of which she was taking full advantage of at the moment.

She poured herself a cup of coffee and sat by the window to study. Her guest had already been prepped and was waiting downstairs in the main dining room, but she wanted to take a few extra moments to review her notes. Under normal circumstances, she would have been fine winging it for an interview, but not this time. This one was too important.

A month after the terrorist incident at the Annenberg, all four major networks began bidding for her services. The month long bidding war drove her salary up beyond anything she could have ever dreamed and she eventually settled on the ABC offer of a weekly news magazine show as her personal vehicle. Of course Alex, bless his heart, wanted her to go work for the BBC or something. Out of respect for their friendship, she pretended to consider it...for a minute.

The ratings for 'Our World Today with Marla Cruz' were through the roof from day one. They consistently trounced all competition in their time slot and she was fast developing a reputation as the best interviewer in the business. Everyone from Hollywoods elite to the political heavy hitters of the day were lining up to sit with her. Simply put, her show was THE place to be if you wanted to get your message out to the public.

After a few moments looking over everything, she knew she was ready. She dropped the folder, gave herself a final wardrobe check in the full length mirror by the door, and made her way into the hallway. As she boarded the elevator, she thought back over the past 18 months since the hostage incident...and smiled. Even Alex, mister journalistic integrity himself, had to admit it was like the gift that wouldn't stop giving.

There were four survivors from the scene shop in the basement, and only one of them had uttered a single word publicly since that night...until today. When she received the call that one of the other survivors was ready to speak, she actually screamed with excitement. When she found out which one, she almost fainted...

The following is a transcript from "Our World Today with Marla Cruz," March 17, 2015. This copy may not be in its final form and may be updated.

MARLA CRUZ, host: Good evening and welcome to the show. On September 11, 2013, I sat in a studio, not far from here, and told you that terrorists had stormed the Annenberg theater in Center City Philadelphia, taking 290 people hostage in what has since been called the most brazen terrorist attack in this nations history. What I didn't know then, what none of us knew, was that 9 people had been taken out of the theater, to a small room in the basement where they were held until police rescued them the next morning. As most of you now know, only 4 of them made it out of that room alive.

In the eighteen months since that fateful night, only one of the four survivors has spoken publicly about what happened inside that room. Now, for the first time, we get to hear another version of those events. Ladies and gentlemen, please join me in welcoming Dexter Swindell to the show. Dexter, thank you for joining us

Dexter Swindell, hostage (survivor): Thank you for having me.

Cruz: Dexter, first let me say, and I'm sure I speak for the entire city when I say this, I'm very sorry for your loss.

Swindell: Thank you.

Cruz: If I have this correctly, your sister Toshia was also your legal guardian?

Swindell: Yes she was.

Cruz: That must have very difficult for you, suffering such a life altering loss at such a young age.

Swindell: Things happen when they happen I guess. Not always when you're ready for them.

Cruz: That's a very mature way of looking at things...

Swindell: Don't get me wrong, it definitely hasn't been easy. I miss my sister every day.

Cruz: People that know you say you two were very close.

Swindell: Toshia will always be my best friend.

Cruz: And she was murdered, in cold blood, by the terrorists who took over the theater that night. How does that make you feel?

Swindell: Sad. Angry sometimes, but probably not as much as you think. I dunno...I'm human, so I guess I feel like anybody would in the same situation.

Cruz: Well, for what it's worth, you seem to be handling your situation remarkably well.

Swindell: Thank you.

Cruz: Other than the loss of your sister, how else has life been different for you since that night?

Swindell: I dunno. I guess I had to grow up quicker, you know? But at the same time, a lot of peoples lives were changed that night, not just mine.

Cruz: But very few people have been through what you have...

Swindell: Maybe not, but that doesn't make me better than anybody else and it doesn't mean what I lost is any more important than what anybody else lost that night...or any other night for that matter.

Cruz: And that's what's so amazing about you and your story. The way you have handled yourself since that night, especially considering your age and everything you've had to deal with, is nothing short of heroic.

Swindell: Thank you for saying that, but I'm not a hero

Cruz: A lot of people would disagree.

Swindell: Well ok, I get that...but just because a lot of people think something doesn't mean its true.

Cruz: Fair enough. But you do realize it's your reluctance to accept the title that makes people so determined to give it to you.

Swindell: I guess...if people wanna think that, thats fine...I just don't think anybody should be called a hero for what we did that night.

Cruz: You referring to Mark O'Connor?

Swindell: I'm talking about all of us.

Cruz: But, before today, Mark has been the only one of the survivors to say anything publicly and, unlike you, he has certainly embraced the whole hero thing...

Swindell: Mark O'Connor is not a hero

Cruz: Can you elaborate?

Swindell: It's like I said before, there are no heroes from that night. Not me...and definitely not him.

Cruz: I assume you know he's running for Senate?

Swindell: Yes, I've seen that.

Cruz: And as of today, he has a huge lead in the polls, so it is likely he will be the next Senator from Pennsylvania in just a few weeks.

Swindell: A lot can happen in a few weeks.

Cruz: So you're not a supporter?

Swindell: I'm just saying there's a lot you don't know...

Cruz: Can you give me an example?

Swindell: I'd rather not get into that right now.

Cruz: Then why say anything at all? You've kept silent all this time and now, out of the blue, you decide to speak up, only you don't want to say anything specific. Help me understand. I mean, is there some kind of beef between...

Swindell: What you have to keep in mind is, when this thing ended, Lena and I had no place to go. We were basically gonna be homeless until Lisa stepped up and took us into her home. Now, Lisa felt like we needed to get our lives back to normal as much as possible, so she didn't want us to speak about that night to anyone. She told us to just put it in the past and, out of respect for her, we did that.

Cruz: What's changed now then?

Swindell: Just because we stayed silent doesn't mean we didn't have anything to say. And when I saw Mark on TV, making speeches and being interviewed, I just felt like it was time for us to be heard.

Cruz: But that still doesn't explain the animosity, which I can only assume stems from something personal.

Swindell: Why do you say that?

Cruz: Because, on paper, there's nothing not to like about him as a candidate. He says all the right things, he is strong on defense and the war on terror...

Swindell: Wait...how is he strong on defense?

Cruz: He is on record saying we should aggressively go after...

Swindell: Kill. By go after, you mean kill right?

Cruz: These are the people that killed his pregnant wife, his father AND, for the record, your sister too. Why shouldn't he want them to pay for what they did?

Swindell: That's not the question. The question is why should we celebrate someone for have a normal human reaction to something? The same reaction any 3 year old would probably have...

Cruz: You disagree with him?

Swindell: I just don't think it takes courage to wanna hurt somebody that hurts you. That's easy. And I'm not saying if someone hits you that you shouldn't hit back. I get that. But I think it takes more courage for somebody to step back while all this stuff is going on and at least try to look at things differently. That, to me , is courage...

Cruz: Is that what you did?

Swindell: Look, are there days where I wanna wild out and blast everybody for what they did to me and my sister? Yes, absolutely...but at the end of the day, none of that is going to bring Toshia back to me or Lena's mom back to her...No matter how many bombs you drop or missiles you launch, they're gone and the rest of us have to find a way to live our lives. That's what they would want...The real hero will be the person who can find a way to prevent any other families from suffering what we did.

Cruz: And you don't think Mark O'Connor is that person?

Swindell: I don't think you can kill your way to peace, no.

Cruz: Is that what you came here to say tonight?

Swindell: I'm here tonight because I wanted to let Mark O'Connor, and everyone else, know that he will not have the last word. The way he sees the world is not the way I see it and I will NOT let him speak for me...

Cruz: Sounds like you're drawing a line in the sand...

Swindell: It is what it is. I just believe there's another way of going about things. There has to be. We can't keep doing what we've been doing and expect something different to happen. We can't just sit by and, because somebody talks tough, blindly follow them down a path that leaves the rest of us behind, scared and hating each other. I don't want anybody else to go through what I did.

Cruz: And you're willing to take on a sitting United States Senator?

Swindell: Like I said, there's a lot about this guy that you don't know. Trust me when I say this, Mark O'Connor will NOT have the last word...

Cruz: Sounds like battle lines have indeed been drawn. Dexter thank you for joining us this evening. I think we'll be hearing a lot more from you in the future...

Epilogue

Marla and Alex were enjoying a quiet dinner at a sports bar downtown. Normally, they would have just had dinner at the Fountain but something about the interview left her feeling uneasy and she needed to get out of there to clear her head. She couldn't quite put a finger on it, but when Dexter left, she wasn't in the mood for the Fountain anymore. She felt like she needed to reconnect with a side of herself she had all but forgotten, so she called her best friend and convinced him to meet her at Champs for some chicken fingers and fries.

"I saw the dailies." Alex said between sips of beer. "The kid was impressive right?"

"Yeah," Marla replied, completely distracted. "That's what I was saying the other day."

"I especially liked when he threatened to choke the cowboy shit out of you if you asked him one more dumb ass question."

"That was good huh?"

Without warning, he took his cloth napkin, dipped it in his water glass and threw it in her face.

"What the hell is wrong with you?!"

"Bitch, you got me out here, at a damn sports bar, on my night off and you haven't heard a word I've said since we got here. What the hell is wrong with YOU?"

They stared at each other for a long moment before they burst out laughing.

"I hate you." Marla laughed as she threw his wet napkin back at him.

"You wouldn't know what to do without me."

"Whatever."

It was the truth, she thought to herself. Alex seemed to always know what she needed and tonight was no different.

"What were you thinking about?" he asked.

"The interview."

"You didn't like it? I thought you killed it and young Dexter was impressive as hell."

"No, it's not that. As far as that's concerned it was fine and I agree, Dexter Swindell absolutely has the 'it' factor."

"Then what's your problem?"

"I don't know...did you get the impression he was hiding something?"

"Like what?"

"I don't know, but I definitely got the impression he was trying not to say something."

Alex thought of responding but stopped himself. Instead, he just smiled at his friend.

"What?" she asked, slightly annoyed that he didn't answer her question.

"So there IS a journalist living somewhere underneath all that Prada huh?"

"Kiss my ass Alex."

"No Miss thing, you are gonna want to be kissing MY ass in a minute."

"What the hell are you..."

"Have you ever heard of Richard Christie?"

"The real estate guy?"

"The billionaire real estate developer, yes."

"What about him?"

"Well," Alex began the story. He'd been planning on approaching her with this on Monday but since she was showing interest he figured he'd better catch her while she cared. "When Mr. Swindell called us out of the blue like he did, I did some checking and you know how he and the other girl went to live with the other survivor?"

"Yea, her name is Lisa Woodward. He told that story in the interview..."

"Did you notice his shoes?" he interrupted.

"Who's shoes?" she responded, getting annoyed. "What are you talking about?"

"Our young friend's." he smiled knowingly. "Did you notice the shoes Mr. Swindell was wearing? They were a five hundred dollar pair of Bruno Maglis."

Alex, I don't give a damn about his shoes."

"That's because you've been wrapped head-to-toe in Versace for so long you forgot how the rest of the world is living. To you, a pair of five hundred dollar shoes is no big deal."

"Whatever Mr. Blackwell." she said dismissively. "I have no idea what the hell you're talking about."

"Exactly." he replied sharply. "Lisa Woodward is a school teacher and before the Annenberg thing, she was single with no children and a live-in boyfriend. Now all of a sudden she is a single mom with two teenage kids."

"What does any of that have to do with what we're talking about?" she snapped.

"Where the hell is she getting the money to buy five hundred dollar shoes?!"

"I could care less where she..." Marla stopped herself mid-sentence.

"You see what I'm getting at?" he smiled.

"Hush money?" she said quietly, still trying to process. "But who? Why"

"Well, I did some digging like I said, and Mr. Christie has made several large donations to the First United Methodist Church in the past 18 months."

"How large?"

"Try fifty thousand and up." he responded proudly.

"And let me guess who is the newest member of First United?"

"One Lisa Marie Woodward, who by the way, grew up catholic and shows no history of ever being particularly religious."

"Ok," Marla said after a moment, her journalistic juices now flowing freely. "so Christie pays off Lisa Woodward, ostensibly to shut her up. Any idea why?"

"No clue." Alex admitted. "But what I did find were not one but two super PACs funded by this guy and I'll give you two guesses who their new golden boy is..."

"Mark O'Connor....wow"

"Wow is right."

"Can we prove any of this?" Marla wanted to know.

"Well, it's easy enough to follow the money. The PAC stuff is public record and the donations to the church you can get from tax records..."

"The problem is connecting any of it to Ms. Woodward," she finished his thought. "And, more importantly, proving why she was paid off in the first place."

Before Alex could respond, Marla noticed something on the TV behind the bar.

"Excuse me," she said excitedly. "Can you turn that up?"

Alex turned around to see Mark O'Connor had just taken the stage to a rousing ovation. He certainly looked the part, Alex thought, dressed conservatively in a dark blue suit, white shirt and grey silk tie. What's more, he seemed very relaxed and confident as he stepped up to the podium. Judging by the footage of the audience, there had to be at least five thousand people there and he absolutely owned each one of them...the guy was a bonafide rock star.

Alex took a sip of his beer and listened intently as Mark began his speech...

"**I** know this might offend the PC crowd but I am not here to make friends. The truth is, they are not like us."

This had become the catch phrase of O'Connors campaign Marla thought as he paused until the applause calmed down. She settled back into her seat and gave her full attention to his speech, suddenly not wanting to miss a single word...

"The criminals that took my wife and father are not only emboldened by kindness, they see it as weakness. We cannot afford to hesitate because this enemy does not understand our compassion. Make no mistake about it, they are not like us!"

The applause grew louder each time he said it, but instead of being impressed, Marla felt queasy. There was something obscene about it, she thought as Mark patiently waited for the applause to subside before continuing...

"They're animals. No, they are worse than animals. They are not men of honor fighting for their freedom. They are cowards preying on peace loving people using fear and violence to advance their agenda of intolerance. NO...they are not like us!"

He was working them into a frenzy like an old pro. It was almost as if he'd been doing this his entire life. And his audience was eating it up like candy.

"Theirs is not a religion of love and peace. They don't serve the god we serve. They don't believe in freedom and they hate us, not because of what we've done, but because of what we have.

You see, ours is a thriving culture of freedom and opportunity while theirs is a failed culture that survives on ignorance and oppression.

As Americans, we are fortunate to live in a diverse and open society. But it is this very openness which is now the biggest obstacle to our security.

Our enemy has a face! He has a name! And to ignore that for the sake of political correctness is lunacy! What the left calls profiling, I call common sense! What the left refers to as bigotry, I refer to as deductive logic!

Those who forget their history are doomed to repeat it and we, at this very moment, are in danger of repeating the mistakes of our past. We cannot assume that because they breath the same air we do that we should give them the same rights and freedoms we have.

Now is not a time for political correctness! Now is a time to protect our children and defend our way of life! You don't negotiate with terrorists. You don't try to understand someone whose stated goal is to kill you. You kill them first. Period.

Now either you stand with us, in this great country of ours, against the animals who want to kill us…or you stand with them.

But make no mistake about it. They are NOT like us!"

As the applause rose to one final crescendo, the bartender muted the volume and poured himself a shot as if he was trying to erase the memory of what he just saw. Marla turned to Alex, who was staring blankly at the screen, unable to put what he had just witnessed into words.

"Stay on top of this." she said after a long moment. "We have to connect the dots on this one."

"I'm on it." he assured her before getting up to use the restroom.

When she was alone at the table, she closed her eyes and smiled. Turns out she was right when she suggested battle lines were being drawn. Only, from the looks of what she just saw on TV, young Dexter had some serious catching up to do.

The kid had the goods. She knew that the minute she laid eyes on him. But he was going to need help, lots of it.

For the first time in years, she knew exactly what she needed to do...

Reading Group Guide

CAPTIVE

A NOVEL BY

Timothy Allen Smith

"It's no longer mine..."

Notes on the cover of *CAPTIVE*

by Timothy Allen Smith

When it came time to discuss the cover of the book, everyone I spoke with couldn't stop telling me how important this step was. Over and over again, I was told I *"had to get this right"* because *"it would be the image that represents your work to the world."*

Well, under this kind of pressure, you can imagine I thought long and hard about what I wanted to do. After beating my head against a wall for weeks and coming up with nothing, I finally realized what the problem was...me. I was never going to get what I wanted for the cover as long as I controlled the creative process.

At its core, CAPTIVE works because of the raw honesty with which we deal with the characters and their issues. And so it became clear to me the cover had to be similarly honest...which means I had to step aside.

From the beginning I knew that, especially with this type of topical material, once the book was released it would no longer be mine. Yes, I wrote the words and yes, I own the copyright, but none of that would matter once people started reading it for themselves. They would read it and dissect it and analyze it and assign meaning to things based on their personal experiences and feelings. All of which is exactly what I wanted to happen. The result however, is once that process starts my direct intentions as the writer would become secondary to those interpretations from the audience. What they felt and what they experienced as a result of reading the book would become the truth while what I intended would be an afterthought. Knowing this, I felt the best way to represent the book was to simply allow that process to happen.

I commissioned Dominy Alderman, an amazingly talented artist, to read the book and create something based on her honest emotional reaction to what she read...all with no creative input from me. I wanted the cover to depict what she felt after reading the book, which I knew would would be a much more authentic representation of the material than anything I could have come up with.

The response to the cover has been overwhelming and I think it's because, like everything else in CAPTIVE, it is raw and honest and makes you want to dig deeper. Book clubs have had entire discussions on the cover alone!

What Dominy delivered is nothing short of incredible and I couldn't be happier with the public 'face' her work has given to my words...

A quick Q&A with the artist

Dominy Alderman

1) Walk us through the creative process you used in creating the cover? Was it easy? Difficult?

This is the first project I have completed without having an initial idea to start. I had a real emotional response to this book. Although it sounds corny, the process started out like a project I would have done in school. I took notes and made a list of all the feelings and emotions I experienced while reading the book. I wrote down certain quotes that really captured my attention like, "just because you're not in chains doesn't mean you're free." I sketched and doodled little ideas here and there in the margins. During this brainstorming phase I even felt compelled to look up the preamble to the Declaration of Independence. I wrote out the first two sections in my notes. I posted these notes right above my desk during the creative phase.

I usually paint to music but for this piece I did not want any external influences to affect the process. I began painting with my hands, choosing bold colors, especially yellow, a color I'm rarely drawn to. The painting was more about appreciating the process, seeing what would be revealed from one step to the next. A black handprint became a part of a skull, alcohol inks became blood spatter. My gender symbol became a cross and an earth, a small field of flowers bloomed among the chaos. Brown horizontal stripes became an opportunity to see flags in the background. A dark circle transformed into the pupil of an eye. The eye being a bit self-reflective; full of shock, fear, and feeling naïve.

I wouldn't describe the process behind this work as easy or difficult. It just was. It was my authentic reflection to the book. There was no plan, no over thinking, just me and a little paint.

2) As an artist, what stands out most about the cover to you?

I'm drawn to the skull in particular because in this context I think it represents the fear of our mortality. When faced with a traumatic event, what is the true character that shows? Or, as Walter says in the book, "it is in a time of crisis that each man shall show his true self..."

3) What did you think when you were told the publisher wasn't going to put the actual book title on the cover?

Pure pride. As an artist I hope to create something that reveals a part of myself that I can't always explain in words. When I look at this work, it truly reflects what I was feeling when I read CAPTIVE, even retrospectively. It's so different from anything I've previously created, and I think it is the best painting I've done.

4) How do you feel the cover best represents what the book is about?

To me, the book is about recognizing all the things that hold us hostage, whether they are figurative or literal. The hope is, in that recognition we can make choices that make US better. It is dark, intense, infuriating at times...and yet in the end we're left with a sense of hope. GOD I LOVE THIS BOOK!!

5) How many versions/ideas did you have (one or many)

I completed five different pieces as I worked on this project. But this was the first "idea" that I had in the sense that I painted without a destination in mind. I think it's by far the most raw and honest, which is exactly what the publishers wanted so it worked out.

Book-Group Discussion Questions:

1) To what extent, if any, did the information about Marks past alter your opinion of him? How would you characterize him? Which situations in the novel reveal what you believe to be his TRUE character?

2) What does Walters' pre-occupation with how much things cost, early on in the novel, reveal about his character later on? In what ways does this contribute to a deeper understanding of him as a person and the things he believes in? Is it a contradiction? Or does it reinforce your opinion of him?

3) Of the relationships depicted in the novel, which would you say was the strongest and why? Which would you say was the weakest or most fragile and why?

4) Which character did you find the most likable in the beginning? Did your opinion change dramatically by the end? Did you find your opinion of any other character(s) changing/evolving as their story unfolded? On which character did your opinion change the most?

5) What assumptions did you, upon reading the prologue, have about the novel and what the story would be about? How did this change as the story unfolded?

6) Looking at herself in the mirror, Lisa is disgusted with what she sees and even comments "Lisa Woodward you are FAT..." but it is also revealed she has no motivation to do anything about it. In what ways, and to what extent, is this a metaphor for the broader world Smith creates in his novel?

7) How did you react to Walters impassioned plea for the others to "look at things a little differently..."? Did you find yourself sympathizing with him?

8) What was your impression of Eleodora's explanation of the American Dream?

9) What is the difference between racial pride and racial superiority? How did the use of racial slurs and epithets in the novel make you feel? What do you think was Smith's purpose in using such language?

10) What does it mean to be a 'race traitor"? What similar terms or labels are used in other situations?

11) How did you feel about Robert and the decisions he made throughout his life? What was the impact of his being "in the closet?" not only for himself but for his family? Do you blame him for what happened? Do you blame society? Both? Why?

12) What challenges does someone who is openly gay face today versus 20-30 years ago?

13) In what ways, and to what extent, did the religious beliefs of each character shape their response the situation? Were the assumptions made about the religious beliefs of the perpetrators fair?

14) What's the impact of terrorism in general, and 9/11 specifically, on the way we interact with each other? Did you find yourself becoming more or less tolerant after 9/11? Was the change temporary? Or was it lasting?

15) Were you personally changed, in other ways, by the events of 9/11? Do you feel any of the characters in the novel went through a similar metamorphosis as a result of 'their' 9/11?

16) Do you believe there is a difference between immigration and assimilation, as Walter put it?

17) What do you think about the way Marla reported on the story of what was happening in the theatre? How is her complete obsession with appearance a parallel for what we get from our own media today?

18) Marla said "In todays world, terrorism equals muslim, period..." How do you feel about a member of the media making such a statement?

19) What impact does the media have on your perceptions and beliefs about people who are from different identity groups than your own? How much of your knowledge about others comes from personal experience and how much comes from the media?

20) How did your own gender stereotypes influence your expectations of who should protect whom, who should be in charge, who should make decisions, what it means to be 'strong', etc?

21) What were some examples of ways the generation gap affected the hostages? Did you find examples in the novel when these age gaps were bridged unexpectedly?

22) How does the definition of family impact our perceptions of ourselves and others? Is a "non-traditional" family structure any less effective?

23) Walter makes the point that "When one black man abandons his family, it effects all of us..." Lisa makes the counter point that "just because a person has the same skin color does not mean everything he does is a reflection of you..." Who do you agree with and why?

24) What are some of the challenges unique to an interracial relationship? Do you feel Walter and Lisa would be able to overcome those challenges? Or do you feel their relationship issues are completely unrelated to race?

25) How were you affected by the profanity? How were you affected by the racial slurs?

26) What language do you use that might offend others, even though it is acceptable to you and your friends?

For more visit:

www.2020Productions.net

www.ingramcontent.com/pod-product-compliance
Lightning Source LLC
Chambersburg PA
CBHW050721180626
46814CB00002B/547